# The Book of Blam

# Aleksandar Tišma

# The Book of Blam

*Translated from the Serbo-Croatian
by Michael Henry Heim*

HARCOURT BRACE & COMPANY

*New York   San Diego   London*

First published in Yugoslavia in 1972 by Nolit, Beograd
This is a translation of Knjiga o Blamu.

Library of Congress Cataloging-in-Publication Data
Tišma, Aleksandar, 1924–
[Knjiga o Blamu. English]
The book of Blam/Aleksandar Tišma; translated from the Serbo
-Croatian by Michael Henry Heim.—1st ed.
p.   cm.
ISBN 0-15-100235-5
1. Jews—Yugloslavia—Novi Sad (Serbia)—Fiction. I. Heim,
Michael Henry.
PG1419.3.I8K5713   1998
891.8′2354—dc21   98-10314

Text set in Stempel Garamond
Designed by Lori McThomas Buley
Printed in the United States of America
First edition
C E F D B

# The Book of Blam

# Chapter One

The Mercury is the most prominent building in Novi Sad. Not the tallest, because it is overpowered by the steep glaciers of the high-rises and the sturdy wreaths of apartment houses that the postwar population explosion strewed over the fields at the edge of town. Nor the most attractive, because its builder and first owner, a prewar businessman, viewed it as a commercial venture, making the most of every square inch and avoiding costly ornamentation. And yet the Mercury, jutting into Main Square, one corner rounded like the stern of an ocean liner, running along broad, straight Old Boulevard in all its four-storied glory (and with its somewhat narrower decklike mansard) and boasting a continuous row of ground-level businesses, including a department store, a cinema, and a hotel with a restaurant and bar, is unquestionably the city's focal point.

Miroslav Blam, who lives in the Mercury's mansard, understands the exceptional, almost lofty status of the building and of himself as a part of it. He is proud of his status, though secretly, reticently so, not having come by it on his own merit. When he writes his return address, he does not use the generally accepted "Mercury Building" (the name comes from the name of the original owner's company); he uses the official though more complicated "1 Old Boulevard," which he also uses when giving his address to acquaintances, and only if they slap their foreheads and say, "Why, that's the Mercury!" does he nod hesitantly, as if yielding to the unofficial, slightly wanton designation, while in fact concealing his pleasure. Or, rather, vacillating between pleasure and annoyance, because he dislikes being pigeonholed, even in so minor a detail.

Actually, the reason he is so fond of his Mercury mansard is that it is in the center of things yet remains a hideaway. Lift your eyes from any point in Main Square or the boulevard and you'll say, "That's where Blam lives." But try to make your way there and find him. First you have to be let into the building or slip past the janitor keeping an eye on the courtyard from his kitchen. Then you have to climb stairs and stairs—four flights' worth, each with dozens of doors and more than dozens of people living behind them, meddlesome people constantly lolling on the balconies—and only then will you come to the mansard level. And are you willing to knock at every door and ask for him? If you're too loud and conspicuous, he may hear you before you find him and thus remain eternally hidden. Yes, even if you do locate the door to his apartment. Because the mansard deviates unexpectedly from the pattern of the other floors, narrowing as it does to the width of a footpath, which, protected by an iron fence so people will not fall to the street, looks like a ship's promenade perched on what is entirely residential space.

Blam often visits this walkway, this place of celestial freedom, slipping out of his apartment through a passage tucked between the laundry room and drying room. Parading thus along the building's edge, he has a bird's-eye view of the Main Square's spacious rectangle and the narrow pointed spire of the cathedral that dominates it, or of the broad trough of Old Boulevard with its endless processions of cars and pedestrians, or of the ravine of narrow Okrugić Street, perpendicular to the boulevard, and the tables in front of the hotel. True, he is so accustomed to these sights that he scarcely notices them, his eye resting rather on an uncommon detail, a lone, dark, pillowlike cloud that seems anchored to the cathedral's spire, or a pedestrian, or a pretty woman who keeps returning to the same place. He pauses at the railing, leaning his elbows on it, eager to take part, to merge with the crowd. He becomes the pedestrian, he becomes the waiting woman. He knows nothing about them, yet for that very reason he can string together images of facts and possibilities. The image of an accident that once took place there, the image of two beaming faces meeting for a tryst. The screech of brakes, a cry of horror that overcomes the crowd like a wind. She is married, but her husband is in jail for corrupting minors and she has phoned an old admirer and asked to see him. The pedestrian hit by the screeching car was Aca Krkljuš's father. Aca himself showed Blam the spot when he gave him his drunken account of what happened. His father's leg was amputated and he could no longer manage his leather workshop, so Aca had to take over and give up his own work and calling. As for the old admirer, he is probably frightened by the responsibility involved—after all, he has remained a bachelor (if he hadn't, the beautiful woman would never have asked to see him): he senses she wants him to replace her husband in the performance of certain familial duties as well as in bed. Aca, or the pedestrian whose choice of position on the street reminds Blam of Aca, seems to be surveying the terrain; he needs to make a sketch of it, a legal drawing, to support his indemnity case, which he has also told Blam about, while the man the woman has asked to see may have got the time and place

3

wrong, mixed things up, because his memory is so poor. But the two people who are actually there waiting will in fact exchange a few glances and hastily thrown-together words; they will grow closer, realize their common bond in the losses they suffered on the same spot. They will begin to trust each other, and he will invite her for a drink or even (because he might well be Aca) suggest they take a load off their feet by going up to see Blam, Miroslav Blam, an old school friend, a friend also of my brother Slobodan, who died a tragic death in the war, Blam always comes to hear my band, my new pieces, he's the one I told about the accident two months ago, the accident that cost my father his leg and me my freedom, he lives right here and he has a wonderful wife, don't worry, I'll introduce you, he's very understanding, and a lawyer, well, kind of, and maybe he can give you some advice about getting your husband off, it's right here, right in the Mercury . . .

A FAR-OFF RING, a knock on the door. Aca with his sagging cheeks, sagging nose, apologetically sagging shoulders, and listless expression suddenly looks amazingly like his dead brother. He pushes the pretty stranger in and introduces her with a quick smile.

"Is Miroslav in?" he asks, winking as if referring to a secret agreement.

"He's around here somewhere," Janja answers, giving him a curious look. "Gone for a walk . . . I'll call him."

"No, no. Don't bother. We'll find him. Just point us in the general direction. We need some legal advice. You see, the lady's husband . . ."

Now they are out again, squeezed together in the passage, because Aca wants to let her go first but also needs to show her the way, and she is rather heavy and afraid the wind will mess up her hair or lift her skirt.

The wind slams a door shut somewhere. Otherwise nothing happens. The two of them are still downstairs in front of the building; up here there is no one but Blam. His fellow tenants avoid the walkway. It is hot in summer and windy at all times. Should they feel the need for fresh air, they go out on the courtyard terrace, where they can drowse, shaded and sheltered, in deck chairs, where they can chat with a neighbor, read the papers, or take the children to play so the children won't disturb afternoon naps. The reason Blam likes the walkway is that he can count on being alone there, at least until someone comes looking for him. Only until then. Because if Aca were in fact to come up with his lady friend, determined to find him, or if there were a search warrant out for him (and eventually there has to be—he cannot imagine living his life without one, without another war), the very fact that the mansard was secluded would turn it into a trap. He would not be able to double back to the terrace: an armed patrol would keep the passage covered. Nor would he be able to duck back into the apartment except through a window: in case of a manhunt, search, raid, or blockade, all windows are closed, all curtains drawn. Those are the rules of the game and have been from time immemorial. All the tenants can do is peek through the blinds, stare wide-eyed and trembling at him out there while a man with a pistol appears in the doorway. Where can Blam turn? His heart is pounding; he presses against the railing, clutching it convulsively, his head bent over the side, his only way out. He refuses to let them corner him again, let them force him to await their orders and to comply; no, he'll jump, he'll swing his body into the air and plunge headfirst into the street as if diving into a swimming pool. He feels a cold stream of air rushing through his mouth, a void enveloping his shoulders, a lack of support, the vanishing borders of space. His legs flop as freely as a rag doll's, they come undone, his whole body loses its shape, its conventional solidity, his blood runs in all directions, everything falls apart, the whole world, the street he is about to crash into.

HIS HANDS TINGLE, his fingers burn, the bar of the railing digs into the bone. He spreads his hands, turns them, observes the red stripes slowly broaden and lose their intense hue. Meanwhile, down below, people keep strolling along the street, going about their business, stretching their legs. The stubborn pedestrian is still there, but the beautiful woman has disappeared; maybe the man she was waiting for actually came. They have no idea what is going on inside Blam; they cannot share it, they would not understand his fear, his terror, his certainty that the patrol will come for him and push him to the railing. What is wrong with him? Is he mad? Or is everyone mad but him? Though it amounts to the same thing. For if he is different from everyone, then he is a monster, a freak, an aberration, ripe for being split open and having his thoughts read, for being crammed into a cage and exhibited in an anthropological rather than zoological garden, exhibited naked, the better to be seen and poked at through the bars until he produces the incoherent howls and shrieks expected of him.

The bars behind him rattle: someone is letting down the blinds. The noise comes from the left, which means it is either the retired woman with bad lungs or someone in his apartment. He does not turn to see, however; he fears the sight he would offer to the person looking out of the window: a twisted head on a body still facing the street, the abyss, with a face showing signs of an overactive imagination, an imagination more real to Blam than anything going on behind his back. Yes, he admits to himself with embarrassment though with a certain malice as well. That intimate world back there, so sure of itself—Janja doing some sewing, perhaps, his little girl doing her homework—is very much part of the manhunt, if not in its service. When passages are occupied, a home like that is disastrous. Any home is disastrous if it is alive, if you depend on it for your life's blood, if you cannot live without it. Then the bullets hit not only you, nor can you even fling yourself to the ground, take cover. There is no cover when you're burdened with love and the patrol is after you. There is no way out. You are being led to the altar to be sacrificed. They push you on, you can't turn back, your head hangs low.

His head hangs low as he waits to hear whether the noise will develop into a challenge, a cry of surprise, a death command. But he hears nothing more, nor has anyone seen him. He slowly turns and, keeping his eyes glued to the asphalt walkway, goes back to the passage. If he can slip through it unimpeded, he will avoid the apartment, the home, the trap, and direct his steps in the opposite direction, the stairs. He will run down the stairs to the street and freedom. He may even catch another glimpse of the pedestrian or the beautiful woman.

# Chapter Two

He does not, of course. They have disappeared in the interim, swallowed by the crowd, or perhaps they are still there but no longer recognizable. People look different when you are on a level with them. The proportions of their bodies change. The relation of one part to another. Formerly conspicuous curves—foreheads, noses, breasts, shoulders—flatten out, and limbs scarcely visible from above jut in all directions. New conditions of light, new reflections affect hair color, eye color, skin color. Clothes seem to hang differently, the new angle accentuating certain wrinkles and shadows while attenuating others. From above, a person's gait looks light and easy; at eye level, it is heavier, involving effort, with one foot always pressed to the ground. From below, it is clear that people are not propelled by an unknown force, not pulled on a transparent string by a concealed hand; they move by contracting their leg muscles and shifting the weight of their bodies in the direction they wish to go. Their connection with the earth is obvious. True, they push away from it, stand erect, but it remains part of them and to it they will return. At eye level, too, their variety—infant, girl, graybeard—arouses curiosity, but the progress of infant and girl and graybeard can be charted from start to finish and their mysteries unraveled.

THE MAN WHO appears before Blam to have his mystery unraveled is a real estate agent by the name of Leon

Funkenstein. Blam sees him while standing in front of the Mercury surveying the far side of the square from the cathedral to the Avala Cinema. The area is full of parked cars because the street beginning behind the Avala and once called Jew Street is now sealed off at the other end by New Boulevard and thus closed to traffic. It is the destination of many idle strollers like Blam.

Seeing Funkenstein, however, Blam interrupts his stroll. He has no reason to avoid him, though he did go out to be alone or, rather, to escape the manhunt, his private term for the onslaught of present and past encounters and experiences, of which Funkenstein is unfortunately a part. He is not sure the old man will recognize him. Blam was still a boy at the time Funkenstein came to the house. But in the past few years, he has given Funkenstein several opportunities to refresh his memory, calling attention to himself with a shy smile, a nod, a barely audible greeting when their eyes meet on a narrow street. But this time there is plenty of room — the whole square beckons Blam to former Jew Street—and Funkenstein stands at the far end of the square bending over the radiator of a dusty gray Fiat, his bald pate so far down that he seems to be sniffing as well as inspecting it.

But as so often happens when he wants to steer clear of someone, Blam directs his steps straight at the man, crossing the square in such a way as to be most visible, justifying his conspicuous route by curiosity. Watching him fiddle with the car, Blam suddenly wonders whether Funkenstein hasn't changed profession. It would be perfectly understandable, given that all rent-bearing properties have long since been nationalized, which leaves only small—and therefore cheap—single-family dwellings on the market like the house the Blams used to own in Vojvoda Šupljikac Square, the one that Funkenstein had sold for Blam's father, Vilim. But he sold it just before Blam's father died, so his father may not have received payment in full, or if he had, then he hadn't had time to spend it all and it had fallen into the hands of plunderers.

He chafes at the thought that he will eventually have to talk to Funkenstein, quiz him on the particulars of the sale of the house to allay his doubts. He realizes he has postponed the talk too long as it is (and postponed putting to rest the doubts), but now he turns his head in Funkenstein's direction and is surprised to find Funkenstein looking straight at him. He can hardly believe it, but there can be no doubt: from the old man's broad, pink face, still lowered over the Fiat's radiator, a pair of tiny but piercing brown eyes beneath unruly gray eyebrows and a shiny forehead are looking at him, Blam.

Blam pauses, whereupon Funkenstein straightens. The straightening does not much alter his spatial relation to the car—he is too short for that—but it does reveal his bold taste in clothes: he is wearing a white shirt with an apache collar over a pair of yellowish imitation-silk trousers. He sets his youthful outfit in motion by circling the car with a sprightly step—surprisingly sprightly for a body so stumpy—and plants himself in front of Blam.

"Hello, Mr. Funkenstein," Blam says, taken aback.

"Hello, hello," Funkenstein answers cordially, but without using Blam's name, which indicates Blam's assumption that Funkenstein would not be able to place him was correct. Funkenstein holds out his firm, fleshy hand, though casually, almost incidentally, and with no more than a glance at Blam's face. "What brings you here?" he asks, clearly aloof and quickly turning his small twinkling eyes from Blam to something over Blam's shoulder.

"Just out for a walk," says Blam, made uncomfortable

by Funkenstein's lack of concentration, which obliges him to keep the conversation going. "Though now that I have you here, I thought I'd ask you about a house you sold a while back. Tell me, are you still in real estate?"

"Oh yes. Yes, of course I am." Funkenstein trains his swift, piercing glance on Blam, but immediately looks over Blam's shoulder again. "Got something to sell?"

"Not anymore," Blam says with a shrug. Suddenly he feels hurt by Funkenstein's indifference and decides to end the conversation, which was going nowhere anyway. "I see you're interested in cars now."

"In one only." Again Funkenstein glances up at Blam, questioningly this time, as if debating whether to trust him. "It's not mine, though. I'm watching it for a friend."

Blam, baffled, turns to see a large green car parked alone in the middle of the square. Suddenly Funkenstein grabs him by the arm and twirls him around. "Don't turn again!" he whispers, raising his wild, imperious eyebrows and pursing his rosy, wrinkled lips, the corners frothy with spit. "I don't want to call attention to myself."

Blam shifts uneasily, realizing that Funkenstein is using his bulk as a shield, that he, Blam, has taken the place of the dusty gray Fiat.

"Look! Look!" Funkenstein cries, triumphant. He is jumping up and down, bending over, peeking out from behind Blam like a child playing hide-and-seek. "See? They're getting on the bus!" Then, suddenly relaxed, he straightens his back and explains offhandedly, "It's a favor for an old friend, a business partner, actually. He's out of town for a while, and I'm keeping an eye on his wife. I knew she was up to something when I saw their car in the square. Well, she's gone off with a man on that bus. To his place, for sure."

From the direction of Funkenstein's gaze Blam can tell he is following the bus (with his eyes or in his mind's eye) that runs past the monument, on to the Danube, and into the part of town filled with new residential dwellings for newly arrived officials, following the dark, young, nattily dressed man and the tall blond woman on his arm, her strong thighs tightly encased in a blue skirt. If Funkenstein's "old friend" is Funkenstein's age, getting on to seventy, perhaps the couple is not so young as Blam imagined. Perhaps the whole thing is a sham. He gives Funkenstein a quizzical look.

But Funkenstein is on his way to the green car in the middle of the square, bypassing Blam as if he were an object. Blam notices that the bus waiting at the monument only a moment before has gone.

"Where did you say your house was?"

Funkenstein has returned to Blam after looking over the car.

"I don't own it anymore, I told you," says Blam, annoyed. "It belonged to my late father. Vojvoda Šupljikac Square, number 7. You were his agent. It was the beginning of the war. I don't know if you remember."

"Vojvoda Šupljikac ... Vojvoda Šupljikac ... ," Funkenstein mumbles to himself, lowering his head and pressing a short, fat index finger to his nose. Suddenly he looks up. "Is your name Blam?"

"Yes. So you do remember."

"Vaguely," he said. "Well, what is it?"

"I was just wondering whether my father ever got the money for the house. The whole sum, I mean. The man who bought it was a tailor. Hajduković, I believe his name was. But then he sold it to somebody else ..."

Funkenstein does not let him finish. "If I was the

agent," he says curtly, placing his hands on his chest and stretching the white shirt, "you can be sure it was paid in full." He gives him a quick nod and holds out his hand. "Goodbye." And off he goes, stepping briskly on his short legs and wide feet in the direction of the monument.

VOJVODA ŠUPLJIKAC SQUARE lies not far from the center of town, in the maze of narrow old streets that now abut on the broad curve of New Boulevard. The houses form an oval around the square, and in its center is a neglected park surrounded by an iron fence with spikes bent out of shape by unruly arms and legs. The land has been so trampled that almost nothing grows there. The few benches are backless, their seats furrowed with lovers' initials that rain has broadened into illegible scars. Only the trees lining the fence have been able to withstand destruction; they are tall and venerable, and their leafy crowns rise above the square like a vast green umbrella.

Blam, too, was a participant in the destruction of this oasis. On his way home from school for lunch he and Čutura would jump over the fence, trample the grass, climb the trees, and eat the berries.

Before he made friends with Čutura, he had no idea that such things were possible or could give pleasure. He had climbed before, but only onto the hand pump of the well in the brick-paved courtyard of his house, where the sole reminder of nature was the flower bed running along the high, bare wall, which broke off abruptly at the separate apartment rented by a widow named Erzsébet Csokonay. The wildest his childhood ever got was jumping from the cold, slippery pump onto the bricks and fighting with his younger sister Estera, which meant a scolding from his mother, or with Puba Šmuk, when Puba's mother came to visit the Blams and brought him along. The house was a fortress under invisible siege. Only relatives, friends of the family, and repairmen came to call—no strangers except for an occasional beggar. Guests could always count on homemade pastries and on fruit brought from the market and carefully washed.

Whenever he took walks with the family, holding hands with Estera (attired in white or navy blue like him) and walking in front of his parents, who kept nagging at them not to stray into the mud, Blam would look at the oval park through the gate, but he never asked the names of the trees that caught his eye by swaying gracefully in the breeze. For Blam a tree was a tree, something big and strong, yet pliant, alive, in cheerful contrast not only to the gray plaster of the street but also to the cartloads of raw, dry timber that arrived at the house at the end of every summer to be hewn into manageable chunks by woodcutters amid the buzz of saws and the smell of shavings and sweat. And while he was vaguely aware that "beech wood" and "oak wood" also came from trees, those trees grew in distant, unfamiliar woods he had never seen and were chopped down by lumberjacks and transported to the city in open freight trains.

Then one day Čutura said, "Hey, let's get some of that fruit!" He jumped over a bent spike between two slanting iron posts and stepped into the bushes. It was about noon and blazing hot, the sun casting its golden lances through the leaves into Čutura's long hair and acned face. Blam followed Čutura's lead cautiously, but caught a trouser leg on the spike. Looking for a place to leave his satchel and free his hands, he saw Čutura's books scattered on the ground in the sun (Čutura had no satchel). But out of habit Blam walked on until he found a shady spot under a tree for his satchel. Only then did he look to see where Čutura was. He found him hanging from the lowest branch of the tree, his open shirt revealing a muscular stomach indented at the belly button. All at once Čutura swung, planted his feet on the branch, and in no time had hoisted himself up. "Catch!" he shouted, throwing Blam three deep-red hawthorn berries still connected by stiff stems. Blam caught them but did not know what to do next, until he looked up and saw Čutura picking more and popping them into his mouth, chewing them, and spitting the tiny seeds out through his teeth. Blam decided to try one. The moment he bit into the berry, a warm, pulpy sweetness flooded his tongue and coated the roof of his mouth. It was like nothing he had ever tasted: it was like chewing spots of sun or a dusty leaf or the rust on the iron fence; it was like eating raw earth, dry and brittle, lying on the earth, burrowing into it. He kept taking fruit from Čutura, popping it into his mouth, chewing it, and spitting the seeds all over, stuffing more and more into his mouth until Čutura grew tired and sprang to the ground, lithe as a cat.

# Chapter Three

If Čutura were still alive, the beautiful summer afternoon might well have lured him out to the square, thus making him a witness to Blam's encounter with Funkenstein. Perceptive, enterprising witness that he had always been, he would have come within earshot and, after their abrupt leave-taking, pressed Blam into a conversation that might have run like this:

"Who was that man?"

"Forget him. His name is Funkenstein. He's a real estate agent. A former real estate agent."

"You were talking about the house you used to live in, weren't you?"

"Right. I thought I'd take the opportunity to bring it up."

"And?"

"You heard. He said he was sure my father had received the full sale price."

"And you never saw a penny of it."

"Right."

"Well, what happened? Or, more to the point, who took it?"

"I haven't a clue."

"You don't seem to have gone out of your way to find out, either."

"I couldn't. I didn't dare, if you really want to know. I

didn't dare inquire after my parents' bodies to say nothing of their money. I was scared."

"Yes. At the time that made sense. But what about later? Have you ever tried to find out who robbed them?"

"How would I do that?"

"How! It seems perfectly simple to me! I mean, it could only have been an inside job. One of the tenants. You must have known that from the start. Remember the Hungarian who moved in with the woman renting the apartment in your yard? What was his name?"

"Kocsis."

"That's right, Kocsis. Well, I used to see him with an Arrow Cross in his lapel. Just the type to get rid of your parents and take over the house."

"How can you say such a thing!"

"Because it's absolutely clear he's the one. He was there the day of the raid, wasn't he? The militia must have asked him about your parents. They used Arrow Cross people all the time. They needed informers. He was perfect for them."

"You're just guessing."

"I'm just being logical. You should have at least looked into the possibility. You didn't do a thing."

"No."

"Which basically means you let those crooks get rid of your parents and grab everything they had. Where are they now?"

"Who?"

"Who! Kocsis and his mistress."

"How should I know?"

"You mean you don't even know that? Did they stay on in the house?"

"I think so. For a while, at least. But then they moved to Budapest. At least that's what I heard."

"So you did ask around! And did a little guessing of your own!"

"Don't be ridiculous. I had to go back to the house to collect what was left of my parents' belongings. It was the new tenants who told me that Kocsis and the woman had moved to Budapest."

"But you didn't find the money."

"No."

"Of course not. The money's what got them to Budapest. They wouldn't have been able to budge without it. But if it hadn't been for the money and the part they played in your parents' death, they wouldn't have needed to move. Can't you see that? They were afraid they'd get caught, so they beat it. They didn't realize they were dealing with someone like you, who wouldn't lift a finger to avenge the death of his parents. They could easily have stayed. They may even have come back. After they saw that nobody was going after them or making any claims and realized the dust had settled. In fact, I'm sure they're back. How much could it have come to anyway? Ten thousand pengö? Fifteen thousand? That's nothing for a bastard like Kocsis who can't hold on to a thing. And when the money was gone and the fling was over, back they flew to the nest. Because I bet they left someone here when they went off on their 'honeymoon.'"

"I don't think she had anybody. Just a daughter, and I'm sure she took her with them. But Kocsis was married, if I remember correctly, and had children."

"Well, then, it's easy. All you have to do is track down the family and get them to tell you where Papa is."

"No, it's not so easy. I never really knew them. I don't know where they lived."

"The Bureau of Internal Affairs has all kinds of records. Might I ask the first name of this Kocsis character?"

"Lajos. His name was Lajos Kocsis."

"I see. Well, it shouldn't be too hard to look up every Lajos Kocsis in Novi Sad. Are you game?"

"Game?"

"To let me take over. I don't share the compunctions you seem to have when it comes to the man. I think his crime cries out for revenge. The people who killed my family had my brothers to reckon with, and this Kocsis is getting off scot-free. I feel it's my duty to do something about it, if only because of Estera, in her memory."

"I don't know. I don't know if it's the right way."

"We won't know until we try. But you can't have anything against my asking around."

"Of course not."

"Good, it's a deal. And you can be sure I'll have something to report before long."

BUT ČUTURA IS no longer among the living, and Blam leaves the square for the former Jew Street, unencumbered by third parties, thinking his own thoughts. As he makes his way along the resplendent shopwindows lining both sides of the street, he feels a venal shudder of regret that Funkenstein would not let him turn and look at the adulterous couple caught in the act. Again he pictures the dark, nattily dressed man and the tall blond woman, her skirt pulled tight around her thighs, pictures them embracing, and realizes it is a goodbye embrace, the repetition of an embrace he witnessed long ago and experienced as a personal farewell.

He experiences it once more, with a bittersweet feeling of loss and withdrawal, though of liberation as well. The memory belongs to memories of the shops now catching his eye. The reality is that the shops have been remodeled, their entrances widened, the cracked wood of the window frames replaced with shiny metal, the merchandise in the windows transformed from aggressive jumbles into neat and expertly arranged displays, the exotic names of owners on the signs supplanted by staid generic terms, the staff supplemented by the young and apathetic ranks of the bureaucracy. It is all quite soothing, a step in the direction of impersonality. It relieves him of the conflict he used to feel when confronted with the dark, tense faces, the rolling eyes, the guttural voices fulsomely praising their wares and humiliating him with reminders of his background. Now the shops, purged of their past, have become for him too places of straightforward buying and selling. I'd like this and that. How much is it? I'll take it or no thank you. Yet he could not help missing the more enterprising tribe to which, even if reluctantly, he had belonged.

The goodbye embrace was similar to—yet in a way the opposite of—the farewell scene he had accidentally witnessed from a tram many years before. Accidentally, because on that day Ferenci, the head of the Úti Travel Agency which had just hired him, asked him for the first and last time to leave his desk and deliver a packet of documents to customs. It was a cold November morning in the first year of the war, and Blam sank against the wooden back of a corner window seat as the tram made its wobbly way toward the customs office. The streets were nearly empty, the morning rush to jobs and the shops being over by then, and all that Blam's absent gaze met as he looked out of the window were a dawdling old man, a housewife rushing home late from the market with her net bag, a postman, an apprentice toting a basket on his back. Then, just before the customs office, where a few small houses huddled together, the tram came upon a couple embracing: a dark man in a gray overcoat and a blond woman in a blue suit. They were standing near the curb, between the tram tracks and the houses, on their own, free, with no one to bother them, leaning blissfully against each other, his swarthy hand resting on her tightly sheathed thigh, her arm over his shoulder, her head and blond hair covering his face. Yet Blam had no trouble recognizing the couple as his wife, Janja, and Predrag Popadić. The realization that she was deceiving him with that man was like a knife in the gut, it took his breath away, it nearly made him faint, yet he did not scream, did not leap up and rush off the tram; he stayed put, leaning against the wooden seat, turning his head to follow them as the tram tottered past. The sight of their embrace on the deserted street filled him, despite his horror, with reluctant admiration; he was almost moved. It was the last embrace of the tryst—he could tell from the way they stood there, from the serenity, the blissful ease of their bodies—an embrace reflecting pleasure and a oneness that came from shared memories of recent intimacy. Joy radiated from them, the joy of oblivion, of having satisfied a natural instinct that, though now abated, still suffused their bodies, the joy of ignoring the world around them, the cold, gray day, the prosaic city with its trams and their troubled passengers. Their joy so vividly contrasted with his grief that for all the pain it caused him he could set it apart and display it like an exquisite object unfathomable in its harmony and forever beyond his reach. He knew then that Janja as she was at that moment, the Janja he had longed for when he was courting her, would never be his, yet the anguish of this knowledge was tempered by relief. By embracing the man out in the open, in the street, she was in a sense taking leave of him, achieving an ideal (even if many years later and with someone else), an ideal that Blam too had yearned for yet never understood and that now proved to be a gentle, sisterly parting, a farewell to a person completely unlike her, alien to her, which would resolve the strain and tension that had always weighed on their relationship, in much the way that the shame and danger of identification with the Jew Street shopkeepers had weighed on him, until they disappeared for good.

BEFORE THE WAR number 1 Jew Street was occupied by a leather goods manufacturing company called Levi and Son. It was run by Levi the son because Levi the father, the firm's founder, was racked by disease and spent all his time in the upstairs apartment with a black silk yarmulke on his head and a tartan traveling rug over his knees. (Levi the grandson was studying to be a pharmacist in Belgrade.) When the Hungarians marched into Novi Sad, they declared Levi the father's leather goods essential to the war effort and carted them away in military vehicles. The empty shop was taken over by Julius Mehlbach, the Levis' longtime apprentice, who turned it into a shop specializing in leather bags and accessories. Levi the son, however, had managed to hide quite a bit of leather in the upstairs apartment, and he offered it to Mehlbach on the condition that they share the profit from the bags made of it. Mehlbach agreed, accepted the leather, and reported Levi the son for concealing goods essential to the war effort. Levi the son was arrested and beaten so badly that his kidneys bled. He was released, but died before the week was up. On his deathbed he summoned Mehlbach and made him swear to care for his all-but-immobile father, promising him a gold coin a week to cover the costs. Mehlbach fulfilled his duty until the spring of 1944, when the old man was deported to a camp in Germany with the rest of the Novi Sad Jews. He never returned. (Nor did Levi the grandson or Levi the grandson's mother, who happened to be with him in Belgrade when the war broke out.) Mehlbach searched the upstairs apartment for the rest of the coins, prying up floorboards and digging behind walls, but never found them, and in the autumn of the same year he was forced to flee the advancing partisans and Soviet Army and thus to abandon the shop and the house.

Number 4 was occupied by a tailor named Elias Elzmann, a refugee from Galicia who had moved first to Germany, then to Austria, and finally to Yugoslavia. His knowledge of Polish enabled him to communicate with his customers, while his wife and grown-up children (who like their father were of heavy build, with oxlike eyes and big noses) spoke only German. For that reason his family—a wife, two sons, and two daughters—did the sewing while he rushed from one customer to the next in a constant sweat, taking measurements, making alterations, bowing and scraping, and lisping all the while in his Slavic mishmash. The Gestapo had the Elzmanns down as German citizens and required the Hungarian authorities to hand them over. They were sent to Serbia, where they perished in the gas chambers. When the Hungarian soldiers went to Jew Street to round them up, they amused themselves by making the Elzmann daughters dance naked in front of their parents and brothers, who had to sing foxtrots and waltzes and clap in rhythm.

Number 3 was the workshop of a small, hunchbacked watchmaker named Aaron Grün. He was commandeered to help clear the rubble from the Novi Sad Airport, had a heart attack, and died in June 1941. His elder son, also a watchmaker, was mobilized in the same year and sent to forced labor in the Ukraine, where he froze to death during the fighting at Voronezh. Grün's younger son, who was still in school and remained at home, was executed together with his mother in the January 1942 raid.

The upper story of number 6 housed the law office of Sándor Vértes. Vértes was a morphine addict, and his wife had tuberculosis. They were childless. Detained as a Communist, he was interrogated and beaten for two days, but was released when he was discovered to be the wrong Vértes. He went home and immediately asphyxiated himself and his wife in the kitchen.

In number 5 a family of well-to-do Zagreb booksellers had opened a secondhand bookshop for their poor hatter brother, Leon Mordechai. After the Hungarian occupation, Mordechai and his family were deported to Croatia, where they ended up in an Ustasha camp. Mordechai's wife and daughter died there of dysentery, but thanks to an early apprenticeship as a tailor, Mordechai survived. Having no reason to return home after his release, he went to Zagreb, where he waited a year for members of his large family to show up or give some sign of life. When none did, he moved back to Novi Sad and joined a hat-making cooperative, where he worked until retirement. He never remarried.

Number 8 was the home of a cross-eyed woman who made bathing suits and girdles. Her name was Elsa Baumann, and she was the widow of a surveyor who died young of neuritis contracted during the First World War. She had one son, a student at the vocational school, who was thin, wore glasses, and had thick, constantly chapped lips. Mother and son were both killed in the 1942 raid.

Number 9 was Ernst Mahrer's laundry. Mahrer had learned his trade in Vienna and was the first to introduce dry cleaning and home delivery to Novi Sad. The van he used had a sun painted on it, with eyes, cheeks, and a smiling mouth. When the van was requisitioned by the Hungarian occupation forces, Mahrer drove it to the artillery barracks himself, parked it in the courtyard, and got out to wait while the papers were drawn up. When the officer in charge saw the smiling sun and the firm's name, he reprimanded Mahrer for not having painted them over. Mahrer responded that that was the least the recipients of the free van could do. Furious, the officer snatched the rifle from the shoulder of a guard, pounded Mahrer with the butt until he fell unconscious, then jumped into the van, whose motor was still running, and ran over him. Word of the incident got around, and the officer was transferred and Mahrer's widow and children ordered to leave Novi Sad forthwith. They received official permission to move to Budapest. In 1943 the son was sent to forced labor in the Bor mines, but escaped and joined the Yugoslav partisans. After the war he remained an officer in the Yugoslav army. Mahrer's widow and daughter were killed during an Arrow Cross show of strength in the Budapest ghetto.

The owner of the shoe shop at number 10 was a methodical, meticulous man named Armin Weiss. A lover of things beautiful and costly—more aesthete than merchant—he was known as far as Budapest for his expertise. Immediately after the occupation a Budapest company offered to make his shop a branch of theirs and let him stay on as an employee. Armed with papers documenting this all-but-governmental commission, he escaped forced labor, which the military authorities prescribed for all Jews; he also survived the raid several months later. But when the Arrow Cross came to power early in 1944, Weiss was deported to Germany with his wife, two daughters, and mother-in-law. None of them returned.

Number 11 was shared by a lamp merchant, Eduard

Fiker, and a stove fitter, Jakob Mentele. Fiker and his family were killed in the raid, while Mentele, a bachelor, managed to survive. He then left Novi Sad for Budapest, where he acquired false documents and lived out the war. After the war he remained in Budapest and died of cancer several years later.

Number 13 housed Arthur Spitzer's grocery and delicatessen. Spitzer played amateur soccer and had non-Jewish friends. Having married a Hungarian and converted before the war, he was spared persecution. He had no children of his own, but his sister sent him her six-year-old daughter from the Independent State of Croatia, where Jews had an even harder time of it. Spitzer held on to his business until the Arrow Cross came to power, and for a while his baptismal certificate, Christian wife, and soccer friends protected him. On the day his young Jewish niece was to be deported, Spitzer and his wife went to the station with her, hoping to save her with their papers and connections. They were all crammed into a train for Auschwitz. There Spitzer was separated from his wife and niece. They all died.

Here is where the former Jew Street came to an end. The section after number 12 on the even side and number 13 on the odd side was torn down after the war to make way for New Boulevard, which intersects the stump of the street with a broad, open, two-way thoroughfare sprinkled with traffic lights. But in the distance, beyond the thoroughfare, its severed extremity—the dot under the exclamation mark—is still visible: a tall, secluded synagogue with Moorish cupolas that is occasionally used for concerts by the Novi Sad Chamber Orchestra or visiting ensembles because of its famous acoustics and absence of a congregation.

# Chapter Four

When houses were torn down to make way for New Boulevard, the part of Jew Street subjected to the sledgehammer and pickax provided unexpected opportunities for observation and thought. As the work proceeded and the buildings lost their roofs, the jagged walls jutted into the sky like scarecrows, then became shorter and shorter—melting away, losing their domestic, human face as doors and windows disappeared to expose undreamed-of twists and turns, mazes like coloring-book puzzles—until finally only the foundations remained, naked and floorless, with gaping chasms where cellar stairs had been and the last walls forming the backdrop for a drama of doom. Standing in parallel rows, shorn of crossbeams, these remaining walls gave the most poignant illustration of the temporary nature of human dwellings: from sky blue to pink and from pink to pale green, with brighter patches of various shapes and sizes representing the beds, pictures, wardrobes, chests of drawers that had stood in front of them, protecting them for years from soot and sun, with here and there a hook, nail, or brace sticking out of their otherwise smooth surfaces. The walls with stubborn magnanimity maintained the tastes and habits of the people who were no longer there; they demonstrated that each house, each room was distinctive, unique, providing each family, each individual with its own way of eating, sleeping, reading, cursing, making love, throwing a fit, and that these different ways of doing things coexisted in amazingly close proximity to one another as well as to what the buildings themselves had kept at bay—the world, the sky, the rain to which they were now pitilessly exposed—and with which they were now becoming one.

BLAM COMES OUT into New Boulevard amid the crossfire of traffic lights and directional signals and the smoke of exhaust pipes. His way is blocked by a light-brown car with a body like a tortoise. It wiggles slowly onto the curb and stops at the very end of the former Jew Street. Blam also stops, instinctively. The back door opens with a click, and out comes a pair of long, tan legs bent at bony knees and a dress hitched up to the thighs. The legs and narrow feet dangle for a few seconds, the changing traffic light reflected on the white sandals; then they alight on the yellow brick of the former Jew Street, knees together, feet apart, spreading spongelike under the weight of the body now rising, head first, out of the open car door. It is a slender body topped by an elongated head with flat features. Protuberant, glassy eyes and sun-bleached hair gathered carelessly in a bun give the face a lifeless quality, yet the woman moves in a lithe, self-confident manner. She stands straight, stretches, and makes a half turn, swishing her slightly wrinkled green dress—loose but belted at the waist—around her bony knees. At the wave of a hand that is as suntanned as her legs, a child's feet in short white socks push out of the door, then the freckled face of a boy with watery goggle eyes appears in the sunlight, and eventually a whole little figure, slightly dazed and distrustful, staggers out into the street and up to the woman. She takes the boy by the hand, which he has automatically held up to her, and looks around. Her pale eyes fall on Blam, run up and down his diffident frame, then wander to the stands selling lottery tickets, books and records, cold drinks and ice cream. Now she motions to the car, completes her turn, and sets off down the street with the child, passing Blam. The other door of the car opens, and a broad-shouldered, thick-necked man wearing a yellowish-brown T-shirt stretched tightly across a hefty stomach twists his way out. He slams the door, thrusts his hands into the pockets of his floppy gray trousers, and walks around the car, examining it with great care. Then, bending all the way down, he takes one hand out of his pocket and feels a back tire (which is be-yond Blam's range of vision), pats the lock on the luggage compartment, and closes the back door. The woman and boy are now at the other end of the street, she slightly ahead of him. No longer holding hands, they are licking ice cream, which threatens to run down the cones onto their fingers. They come to a halt in front of the man but do not so much as glance at him, their attention riveted on the progress of their tongues along the smooth pink mounds. They lick the now-flattened top of the ice cream, then nibble on the soggy edge of the cone. At one point the woman mutters a few words and purses her lips in the boy's direction, and he, following her glance, lowers his protuberant eyes to his stomach, where the hem of his white shirt has come out of his tight shorts; but, having found nothing out of the ordinary, he goes back to licking, nibbling, swallowing. Before long their hands are empty, and they stand there staring at their idle, sticky fingers. The woman says something to the man, and he takes his other hand out of his pocket along with a crumpled hand-kerchief, which he hands to the woman. She unfolds it, wipes her fingers, then bends down and wipes her son's,

tucking in his shirt while she is at it. She returns the handkerchief to the man, who examines it, folds it up, and stuffs
it back into his pocket. All three lift their faces and squint
at the sun, which, though not visible, sends its rays down
between the gables to form a triangle on the gray dusty
street, a gold-plated layer of dust. The man walks around
the car, opens the front door, and slowly, rocking the car's
body with his bulk, squeezes behind the wheel. Then the
woman opens the back door, picks the boy up under his
arms, and, bending, swings him onto the seat. She watches
him make himself comfortable in the corner, then turns
toward Blam (that she sees him without seeing him is reflected in the harmony of her movements), and withdraws
first her body and head, then her legs, knees together, into
the car. The front door, then the back door clicks shut. The
engine turns over and starts humming, and the car rolls
slowly back off the curb and joins the stream of traffic
moving along New Boulevard.

Blam sets off in the same direction—here the sidewalk
is nearly level with the boulevard's asphalt surface—past
the rear walls of the houses left along the former Jew
Street. On one side he is whipped by the wind of the
speeding cars and on the other soothed by the peeling plaster and pink-and-yellow bricks. The memory of the family
that emerged from the car to act out a scene of their life for
him is still fresh in his mind; he goes over the way they
moved and gestured. But the houses he is passing also
claim him—their proportions and materials, their stains
and scratches so long familiar. One side of the street is the
past, the other the present. He can't get at the present, he
knows he can't, though he feels it, feels it bodily, on his
skin, like the sporadic gusts of air from the boulevard that
lash him and move on, carrying off group after group of

people like those he has just seen. He knows he will never sit behind the wheel of a car he is both owner and master of and give himself up to the wind, the speed, taking along Janja and the Little One, who would have no trouble adapting to and merging with a strange city, a strange country. He lacks the self-confidence or the energy for it; nor does he feel the need. His will dooms him to return to the same old roads and streets, to remain their intent yet listless and melancholy observer.

New Boulevard forms a kind of bow arching through the remains of a once-lively community. The sidewalk narrows at the corner of a garden wall forgotten during the demolition process, then branches away from the houses to a side street. Blam passes the wall, enters a narrow alley, and, proceeding to its end, comes out into Vojvoda Šupljikac Square.

The square looks as it has always looked, its houses silently embracing the small park. There is no motion but the gentle sway of the spreading hawthorns. There are no pedestrians. In front of a gate two houses down from Blam's former house, an old woman sits on a low stool, her gnarled hands crossed in her lap, her jaw moving. At first Blam thinks she is chewing, but as he gets closer, he realizes it is an illusion, her jaw is moving for no reason or else out of boredom or pain. The bowl full of peaches in front of her is untouched. She is selling them here in the empty square, having picked them in her garden, a cramped space behind her modest house, or in her daughter's garden, or in the garden of a neighbor who does not care to expose herself to the street's prying eyes. The old woman is patiently offering the peaches at a price below what the market is charging, in the hope of making a little extra money.

Blam has to stop; his legs force him to, as if he too were

old, ailing, and exhausted from long waiting and hope. Gravity pulls him down, down to his knees, to touch the ground with his head and weep, not for the old woman's fate, for her thankless, hapless undertaking, her sacrifice; no, for her faith, which keeps her here by the gate, by the bowl of fruit. Blam sees her faith as the faith of a world now gone, a world of which he too is a remnant. That faith has proved pitiful, futile, because the people who lived by it have all been murdered and forgotten, erased by time and asphalt roads, and he is its last witness, the only person able to appreciate and interpret it, but only for himself. The old woman cannot, though she has survived and preserved that faith. She may even belong to those who did the killing or who looked on in silence while the killing went on or who thought the killing justified. But at this moment she personifies for Blam the now defunct world of ardent faith, and through her he returns to it, to the faces of the departed tradesmen and brokers of the former Jew Street, the faces of his parents and sister and other relatives, the faces of friends who sinned against him and friends whom he sinned against.

"Come with us!" Lili said or, rather, "Komm mit" in her guttural, voluble German, because she never learned Serbian or cared to, which infuriated Blam. Nearly everything about her infuriated him: her garish way of dressing and behaving, the sarcastic look in her multicolored eyes, the panache with which she paraded around provincial, patriarchal Novi Sad, swishing her willowy dresses and addressing everyone in loud German as though it were perfectly natural for them to speak her language rather than for her to speak theirs. "Eccentric" was the way he thought of her, not realizing he had taken the word over from his mother, and after possessing her physically and thus emotionally and intellectually, and feeling a need to correct and torture her, he used it openly with her: "You're an eccentric. No one can live life the way you picture it." But she would just open her greenish-brown eyes wide with amazement and turn the ends of her mouth down into a pout or up into a sneer, which then spread to the dimples in her cheeks and to the smooth expanse of her forehead. While she never protested, she never seemed to grasp the point of his reproaches; she simply waited until he got them out of his system so she could snuggle up to him with one of her "eccentric" demands: "Kiss me quick!" "What I wouldn't do for some chocolate!" "I want to go dancing!" "How about a film tonight?" And "Come with us!" He would say no, routinely, more out of spite than conviction.

The only thing he always agreed to was meeting her in their hideaway, a room he had sublet in remote Dositej Street at her instigation, though what Lili offered him was a mixed blessing and even cause for regret. To begin with, the widow he sublet the room from made him uneasy. She was a tired, lifeless woman who may have believed what he said when she rented him the room facing the courtyard with a separate entrance—namely, that he was a student from the countryside—but was then doubtless shocked to find the room locked day and night and to see the young man only on hot afternoons and always with a thin young woman whose arms, legs, and skirt were in constant motion and who never stopped chattering in her strange, incomprehensible language, not even after her green lover let her into the room. He suspected the widow would have thrown him out if she had been less worried about the expense involved in running another advertisement and the energy involved in showing the place again, and as a result he was full of remorse for living a lie and getting away with it, and that remorse poisoned his feelings for Lili. He upbraided her for flaunting their mutual lie the way she flaunted her loud dresses, loud laugh, foreign language, and even more foreign origins.

Shame and spite made him reluctant to follow her on the next leg of her journey, her migration through Europe, this time to Italy, where her father was to sell an invention of his. Ephraim Ehrlich was always bragging; for him, reality and bragging were indistinguishable. Here too, in Novi Sad, he made his living—feeding and clothing himself and his daughter and renting an expensive furnished apartment—more by blowing his own horn than by applying whatever technical knowledge he might have had. He carried on lengthy secret negotiations with greedy, gullible Jews about the advances he needed to develop and perfect the inventions that would bring them millions. "He's a sharp one, that Ephi," Vilim Blam would say approvingly, lounging in his armchair and clenching a cigar in the strong, white teeth he was always quick to flash. An Ehrlich on his mother's side, Blam's father liked to think of himself as cast in the same spirited mold, as "a sharp one." He was in favor of Miroslav's going with his relatives, not because he saw the danger of persecution and extinction drawing closer to Novi Sad (his faith in people and in his own good fortune precluded all possibility of danger) but because he felt that moving away, a change of scene, would provide his son with greater opportunities in life. "Oh, to be young again!" he would sigh, throwing his head back on the antimacassar, patting his stomach with a soft, fleshy hand, and puffing white smoke rings that filled the dining room and said that he did not in the least wish to be young again, that he was perfectly content as he was, with a well-fed body and a cigar between his teeth. "I'd grab the opportunity," he would say, making a fist, as if he had the opportunity right there in his hand.

Ehrlich would sit opposite Vilim Blam with his hands folded on the table—he did not smoke—and nod approval. He tended to be serious, formal. His narrow face and strong features made him look more like a pastor than an inventor, and his bright blue eyes and thin lips made him look utterly different from Lili, whom he adored, perhaps for that very reason, as she adored him. His speech was slow, monotonous, and dry but so effective that one felt compelled to listen. He maintained that the Jews of Novi Sad, Blam included, were making a big mistake by ignoring the experience of those already threatened and destroyed. He cited the example of friends from Vienna who had sat twiddling their thumbs until the Nazis threw them out of their factories, shops, and apartments, and then, after robbing them of their money and connections, sent them off to camps and starved them to death. "'What are you waiting for?' I said to them. But they stayed put. They didn't listen. And you know why? Because they had no faith in themselves, because they thought they couldn't live without their Persian rugs and crystal chandeliers." Then Ehrlich would give detailed descriptions of the contents of vacant Jewish houses and the plundering of the valuables, and Blanka Blam, who was fanatically devoted to hearth and home, trembled with horror and threw her husband desperate glances begging him to restrain his relative, for Ehrlich was very much his side of the family, and she secretly believed that her much stricter clan could never have produced so merciless an observer, though how could the man be otherwise with no real profession, no real home, how could a man widowed at such an early age fail to marry again, how could he bring up that child, that Lili, on his own, letting her do whatever she pleased, letting her seduce the boy in front of everybody?

Lili did in fact seduce Miroslav. To persuade him to leave, she did not use her father's tactics of referring to horrors suffered and witnessed; instead she flattered him, yet gave him reasons much like his father's. "What's a man like you going to do in this dead end of a town?" she would ask, looking at the nearly deserted streets of Novi Sad, though she seemed to be having the time of her life there. "A smart, handsome, capable man like you? Why, you're made for the world!"

Blam was embarrassed by her praise, but it made him feel capable in her presence, even handsome. It made him wiser and deeper. He parried Lili's arguments with bitter, proud sobriety: Yes, he realized he could expect a vain, futile existence here, even degradation and death, but he saw no reason to try and escape his fate. "Life has no meaning anyway," he would say. And, "Life is pure illusion."

If Blam himself was surprised at the bleak maturity of his pronouncements, Lili was enchanted by them, and much as she protested in fact, they were precisely what she wanted. Though the same age as Blam—and therefore, as a woman, considerably more mature than he—she was certain he knew more about love. Once, when they were still getting to know each other, she spun around and, peering up at him to see how he would react, came out with "I have a fiancé in Vienna, but I don't know if he's alive." Which set Blam off on a jealous disquisition about how senseless it was to keep a relationship going after the bonds of attachment had come undone: she was like a child holding a broken kite string. "Oh, how right you are!" she cried contritely and threw her arms around his neck. They were in

Vojvoda Šupljikac Square (whose name she always replaced with a laugh, never able to pronounce it) after one of Blanka Blam's abundant meals, having left the grown-ups and lazy Estera to digestion and serious talk. "Kiss me!" Lili said for the first time, standing on her toes and pressing her small, firm breasts into his body. "Somebody might see us!" Blam replied, flustered yet managing to sound prudent and reasonable, so that Lili had to say, "But there's nobody here!" the truth of which Blam confirmed with a cautious glance. "All right, then," he said and lowered his mouth to her thin, burning lips, which quickly sucked it in. Her whole body trembled, twisted, and in the end she burst into tears. "I can't betray Hans. He's in a camp, and at this very moment they may be torturing or killing him!"

Yet she was the one who came up with the idea of renting a room, and she was so excited when she first saw it that she immediately threw off her clothes and lay down in the huge, cold peasant bed. She squeezed her eyes shut as he entered her clumsily, her face contorting, her forehead breaking out in sweat, because she was a virgin, and when it was over, she jumped out of bed with the sheet wrapped around her and ran to the basin, head held high, to wash the blood off. Her naked body was firm and slender and had a honeylike sheen. She was not ashamed of it; indeed, she flaunted it by making more trips to the basin than necessary.

"Do you like the way I look? Tell me!" she asked with a smile, unaware that by so doing she was spoiling the way she looked. Blam felt there were certain things a person did not talk about, one of them being whether a person liked the way another person looked with no clothes on. Before long, however, he was forced to talk about other things a person did not talk about: after their third tryst Lili told him she was pregnant.

She was very brave about it, even defiant, announcing before Blam had a chance to say anything that this was "no time for weddings and babies." Nor, to Blam's great relief, had she any intention of letting her father in on the secret: it would only cause him distress and divert him from his highly demanding work. Still, the unwanted fruit of her womb could not be removed without some assistance from the older generation, so after much hesitation Blam confessed everything to his mother. Though stunned, Blanka was the only one who had foreseen the possibility of the tragedy and immediately went to her husband. Vilim Blam took the news calmly; he even seemed proud that his son had taken a mistress at so tender an age, and he was not the least perturbed by his son's having chosen a relative. He was therefore perfectly gallant about getting the money together and even invited Lili to Vojvoda Šupljikac Square for three days, telling everyone that it was in celebration of her impending departure. She left the house on foot accompanied by Blanka Blam and returned with her in a carriage, pale and visibly thinner than she had been two hours earlier yet smiling as ever.

Lili convalesced in the dining room, fully dressed but lounging on the sofa in Estera's soft slippers, listening to the radio, waited on by Blanka and Estera, both of whom were moved by the event. The men of the family gave her a wide berth, but Ephraim Ehrlich would blithely enter the dining room, kiss his daughter on the forehead, not noticing or pretending not to notice her mysterious condition or loss of weight, and launch into a monotonous exposition of current events, of his achievements and plans, of their departure. After the discovery of and embarrassing epilogue to the incestuous relationship, no one gave another thought to Miroslav's going with them. Even Vilim

Blam stopped bringing up the subject, having most likely realized that a seventeen-year-old is not old enough to live abroad on his own, and Ehrlich seemed to know more than he let on. Only Lili kept begging Miroslav to come with them, painting life abroad in the brightest colors and promising she would let him enjoy it: he had only to say the word, and she would give him complete freedom. But after what he had been through, Blam had lost the desire— or the courage—to throw in his lot with her; in fact, he could hardly wait for her to go. Still, he selfishly yielded to her pleas and took her back to the Dositej Street room several times, though now taking the precautionary measures he had failed to take earlier. Otherwise he avoided her. He had the feeling that her early pregnancy was merely another of her eccentricities and that a life with her would be full of absurd and disagreeable consequences. He heaved a sigh of relief as they parted, she bathed in tears, at the dreary Novi Sad railway station. Her bags, having been purchased in the various countries of her exile and therefore of all shapes and sizes, were like the magnificent finale of a visiting circus, after which life goes back to normal.

# Chapter Five

Blam spends his mornings at the Intercontinental. He sits there like a bump on a log, like the fossil of a long forgotten age. Which he in fact is, having been blown there by the wind of an extinct climate, the harsh, merciless, climate of the Occupation, though it was slightly milder for a Jew who had converted to Christianity and married a Christian and was therefore exempt from annihilation.

In those days the Intercontinental was still a minor branch of the Budapest-based Úti Travel Agency. Since Hungary was at war and her borders were closed, it dealt entirely in local train and bus lines and had only two ticket counters and two desks in a single Main Street office, and it was here—in the farthest corner, in the penumbra of accounts payable and outstanding correspondence—that Blam holed up, hoping to escape the public eye and ill will. Although this imposed isolation made him something of a martyr, although the stamp of martyrdom meant he could welcome the change in regime with open arms and a clear conscience (he and he alone remaining, all the other employees—starting with Ferenci, his boss—having fled), or perhaps for these very reasons, the Intercontinental even in peacetime was still a place of seclusion, depression, and alienation for him.

All that had changed were the externals: the witnesses and agents of his condition. After the enterprise was reformed and restructured in the postwar period, it was headed by Slavko Jurišić Juriš—former partisan, former municipal clerk, and former student of theology—whose virile allure, significantly enhanced by the gun at his waist, attracted half a dozen girls from newly founded patriotic organizations. The premises proving too small for so large a staff, Jurišić gradually expanded the operation (which municipal headquarters voted to give its new, internationalist name) by requisitioning apartments in the back of the building. And whether Jurišić had intended it or not, the newly converted office space led in turn to an expansion of the Intercontinental's activities: before long it was dealing in all kinds of travel and tourism, with a bevy of pretty and accommodating women behind glassed-in counters and, in the background, an army of glowering administrators, bookkeepers, and drivers.

Blam, the longest witness of the growth, follows it with distrust, a distrust that grows in proportion to the general increase in demand for travel, action, change in a world drunk on peace. The son of the enterprising, devil-may-care Vilim Blam, whether from bitter family experience or out of rebellion, tends toward severity and moderation, so whenever the Intercontinental is about to take a risk on a long-term group of package tours, say, or the purchase of a vehicle on credit, he feels wary, close-fisted, and if anyone asks his opinion, he will advise against it and predict the direst of consequences. But package tours are the rage, and with more and more money in circulation, interest rates have gone down. Bitter, almost disappointed, Blam retreats. The lack of moderation on the job and in society at large is at odds with his nature. He refuses to take on complex tasks, sticks to billing and filing at his old desk off to the side, out of the limelight, and plods his stubborn way through boring work.

Jurišić, who has a soft spot for Blam because they have

worked together since the beginning, is concerned. "Poor old Blam," he says, sighing a gently reproachful sigh and giving him a warm, anxious look. He sits down opposite the calculating machine, no longer in uniform or carrying a gun but with a heavy coat over his shoulders, having been plagued for years with an inflammation of the kidneys. "You don't understand how things work nowadays," he says in the intimate tone he uses only with Blam. But when Blam merely shrugs his shoulders, Jurišić's concern gradually blends into confession and ends in self-pity. "Maybe you're right to act the way you do. You've got your peace of mind, and that's what counts. Look at me! I'm a wreck!" He launches into laments over how much work he has and how bad his health is. Then, encouraged by Blam's silence, he delves into the complications of his private life, which Blam, alone among the employees, can grasp immediately, having witnessed how they came about. "The witch has sent me the kids again." The "kids" are the children from his first marriage, which fell apart when, in the process of taking over the office with pistol still at his side, he set his sights on one of the ticket-counter girls. Now he is supporting both women, and both are always demanding more. "You've got a nice, quiet life. Not very exciting, maybe, but no problems."

Blam nods. Then, confused, he shakes his head: he doesn't want it to seem that he is confirming Jurišić's problems. Blam's problems are nothing like Jurišić's—they are not nearly so obvious and tangible. What gets Jurišić into trouble is his willful character (something Blam has never had to worry about). Blam pities him. No, admires him. Admires his impetuosity, his refusal to acknowledge hardship and danger, his impulsive decisions, his disregard for the voice of reason and doubt. In the man's simple-minded rashness Blam feels a power alien to him, the power of risk-taking; he feels an animal warmth emanating from Jurišić and engulfing him, especially when Jurišić opens up to him so completely and about such intimate things. As miserable, ill, shivering, and jaundiced as Jurišić is, he draws Blam in, draws him to the oneness of people who think and feel alike, who belong to the same generation and share its experiences, and eventually to the oneness of all people living on the planet.

It is this intimacy that has kept Blam at the Intercontinental through the years despite the burden of past associations and his disapproval of the way things are run there. He has nothing else. The fact that Jurišić sits down at Blam's desk to let off steam when he quarrels with his wife or gets a warning from the courts or discovers a new pain, the fact that employees on their way to Bookkeeping remark how cold or dark or smoky it is at Blam's desk or request a piece of information only he can provide, the fact that the typists and clerks congregate not far from where he sits hunched over his papers, sip their coffee, and discuss their dressmakers or the prices they have just paid for the meat or fruit bulging out of their net bags, not noticing that they are disturbing him and blocking his light, the fact they do not notice not noticing him, which means that they accept him, take his presence for granted, take it as a real and logical thing, the only possibility at that place and time—none of this is a source of annoyance; it is a source pure and simple, a stimulus pure and simple, a way of feeling something genuine, concrete, vital. It is a stimulus that keeps Blam from considering himself invalid or unnecessary or nonexistent.

BLAM SPENT HIS school years between Aca Krkljuš and Ljuba Čutura. A coincidence? Yes, but like any coincidence not without its reason. Though tall, Aca Krkljuš had ended up on the second bench, to Blam's left, so that he could be near his elder brother, Slobodan, who was a year behind because of a hearing problem and had been given a seat up front. Čutura sat to the right of Blam—they were separated only by the space between the desks—because the two were approximately the same height. In any case, this coincidence corresponded to a certain reality, the absentminded and solitary Blam representing a kind of transition between the musical, restless, loose-jointed Krkljuš and the slow but steady, thoroughgoing Čutura. If there was anything extreme about Blam's character, it was in the affection he felt for both friends.

In their fifth year they had a Russian-émigré German teacher by the name of Yevgeny Rakovsky. Rakovsky was short, thin, and of a sickly constitution, and he wore thick spectacles that made him look bewildered. He nonetheless strutted about the classroom, back straight and head high, and if, carried away by his motion and deceived by his glasses, he bumped into a bench or tripped over the podium, he would turn pale, regain his balance, puff out his chest, fling his narrow head back, and burst into raucous, broken, nervous laughter. What was he laughing at? Himself or the obstacle he had overcome? No one knew. In any case, the class would take advantage of the opportunity for a break and loudly second their teacher's laughter, laughing to the very limit of decency.

But Rakovsky gave his students a more generous and more regular break from work: his talks. After a quick and thorough presentation of the material for the day—he had an excellent command of German, though he pronounced it in the soft, Russian way, as he did Serbian—he would clasp his hands behind his back, thrust out his chest, pace back and forth in front of the podium, stumbling now and then and spurting the occasional jet of laughter, and sermonize in his shrill, piercing voice. He spoke of the crisis in Slavdom, whose most powerful branch, Russia, was being eaten away by the Bolshevik blight, an ideology of mediocrity and ignorance designed to bring about Russia's downfall, an ideology sown by the Jewish nation, which was scattered around the world and which, like all parasites, fed on healthy plants. To combat the evil, he preached a new, militant society based on ancient Sparta, one that promoted might, bravery, and determination and discouraged softness and weakness as breeding grounds for the plutocratic Jewish plague.

Encouraged by both the attention of his audience and the obvious successes of the Spartanlike military regime in Germany, Rakovsky gradually intensified his rhetoric. Blam was understandably uncomfortable. Whenever Rakovsky came to the end of the brief question-and-answer session after the grammar lesson, folded his hands behind his back, and pulled his puny frame up to its full height, Blam, in his isolation (he was the only Jew in the class), felt cramps in his stomach, the blood draining from his head, and a stabbing pain in his chest, and while he suffered, his classmates heaved a sigh of relief, their faces all smiles in anticipation of a good time.

The nightmare was in no way mitigated by the fact that Rakovsky did not attack Blam personally. He evaluated Blam's class performance fairly, even overlooking minor errors: his preoccupation with general principles made him in most respects a fair-minded teacher. But Blam sensed that behind the lack of personal malice lay the patience of a fanatic circling his victim with feigned indifference while waiting for the right moment to pounce. Blam found evidence for the circling in the fact that whenever Rakovsky did lose his temper, he aimed his barbs at Blam's neighbor, Aca Krkljuš, though it must be said that Aca gave him plenty of ammunition, coming to school half asleep, failing to do his homework, not even knowing what lesson they were on, the very opposite of his deaf and dull-witted but industrious brother, and when Rakovsky discovered that Aca went in for jazz, he started singling him out in his talks as a degenerate Slav. At the same time, Rakovsky made Čutura, Blam's other neighbor, his pet, addressing him personally from the podium, as if wishing to separate and shield him from Blam's evil influence. The choice of Čutura as a pet demonstrated even more than did the trips and falls caused by his poor eyesight Rakovsky's inability to grasp reality, because Čutura (whose real name was Ljubomir Krstić, though all the students and even all the teachers other than the infatuated Rakovsky called him Čutura, "brandy flask") was even then a committed Communist—an unambiguous, provocative, self-confident Communist, whose older brothers were both known revolutionaries in town. But Rakovsky, isolated from the rest of the population by his in-the-clouds ideas and from the rest of the teaching staff by his unpopular political stance, failed to realize not only that in Čutura he had an ideological enemy but also that in Čutura's pointed, robust simplicity and stoic hostility he had the very type of strong-willed young Slav he called for in his talks. Čutura did no better at his lessons than Aca Krkljuš—he simply had no time to take them seriously—yet Rakovsky gave him high marks for the most superficial answers and accepted anything he said to justify his absences, which were many, for Čutura attended every illegal meeting he was invited to.

Blam occupied a middle position between Krkljuš and Čutura in the matter of Rakovsky's respect as well. But he was instinctively aware of the fragile quality of that position, and he feared the day when its equilibrium would be upset. When the day came, after a year or more of teetering, Čutura was the cause.

Rakovsky, in his usual precise manner, had asked Slobodan Krkljuš to conjugate an irregular German verb, but his Russian accent was too much for the hard-of-hearing Slobodan, who looked up at Rakovsky's lips with a good-natured smile and asked him to repeat the question. Rakovsky was happy to do so. A cornerstone of his pedagogy was: If you don't understand, don't be afraid to ask. But just as he was about to formulate the question more distinctly, Aca Krkljuš, who had been hunching behind his brother, afraid he would be next if Slobodan got the answer wrong, leaned over to Blam and begged for the verb forms with his eyes. Blam whispered them to him, but he was too loud and Rakovsky heard him and took it for an attempt to help Slobodan.

"Blam!" he screeched, as if he had just been scalded, his head jerking forward, his clenched fists falling to his sides.

Blam stood up.

"What did you say?" Rakovsky croaked.

"Nothing to him," Blam answered, flustered.

Either failing or refusing to understand what Blam meant, unable to accept anything but lies and treachery from Blam (perhaps for some time now), Rakovsky flinched at these words as at a leper's touch.

"What did you say?" he repeated shrilly, his face red, his lips twitching.

Having to pass Slobodan's desk to get to Blam's, he bumped into it on the first step, but instead of laughing as usual, he bared his crooked teeth, regained his course, and moved on with short, clipped steps, holding his head high like a soldier on parade, except that his features were convulsed with hatred, his eyes were smoldering and his thin, curled lips were spotted with foam. He stumbled once more in the space between the desks, but undeterred, lifting his fists and waving them over his head, he made for Blam.

Suddenly Čutura rose from his bench and positioned himself by Blam's desk. He stood there calmly, arms at his side, his composure making it clear he would not budge. Rakovsky sensed as much and hesitated for a moment, but then a hoarse sound emerged from his throat: a whimper or muffled cry. He was so much shorter than Čutura that when he got to him, his raised fists barely reached Čutura's slightly furrowed brow.

"Don't do it, Professor Rakovsky," Čutura said firmly.

Rakovsky flinched again, his lips curling. Then he turned to Blam, as if to find a way past the obstacle and do what he had set out to do.

Čutura took a step backward in Blam's direction.

"Don't do it, Professor Rakovsky," he repeated in the same firm but quiet voice.

Rakovsky turned to him, his eyes bulging as if he had received an electric shock, his white fists shaking above his head, his mouth twisting, his breath hissing. Then all at once something snapped inside him, and he threw back his head, opened his mouth, and burst into his broken wheeze of a laugh. The class, mute from the suspense, was slow in joining him, but once he lowered his arms, the fearful, obsequious sputter grew into a roar. Rakovsky then executed an about-face and returned straight-backed to the podium. Čutura motioned to Blam to be seated and slipped silently back on to his own bench. The class resumed.

ČUTURA IS CRUISING the city. He may be wearing a sweaty shirt unbuttoned at the chest, he may be wearing a suit and tie and driving his own car, depending on the position he would have had in postwar society. One thing is certain: he is carrying a list of all the Novi Sad Lajos Kocsises in his pocket, a list consisting of addresses alone, the names being the same. Čutura is gathering new, postwar evidence of diversity beneath apparent uniformity.

"Does Lajos Kocsis live here?"

"What do you want him for?"

"I just want to talk to him. Is he in?"

"If it's about money, you might as well leave now. Half of his salary goes to pay off his loans. And the three kids you see here? He's their sole support."

"Are they his?"

"They're mine, comrade, and I won't let anybody take a crumb away from them, understand?"

"The Kocsis I'm looking for is an old man. I think they gave me the wrong address. How old is your husband?"

"Who gave you my address anyway?"

"A common friend. I'm trying to give him money, not take it from him. Is that him in the picture with you and your children?"

"Yes, it is."

"Then I apologize. Please forget I ever came."

"Does Lajos Kocsis live here?"

"Yes."

"Where is he?"

"Sleeping."

"Are you related?"

"I'm his mother-in-law."

49

"Can you tell me if he ever lived in Vojvoda Šupljikac Square?"

"Where? Wait a second. Marta! Marta!"

"What is it?"

"This man wants to talk to Laci."

"I'm sorry, ma'am. I may be wrong. I'm looking for a Lajos Kocsis who moved to Budapest during the war. Could that be your husband?"

"My husband was in Budapest during the war. In the army. What do you want from him?"

"The Kocsis I'm looking for went to Budapest as a civilian with a woman who lived in Vojvoda Šupljikac Square."

"What are you talking about? They took him against his will and he came back with his legs cut off. Mother, can't you see the man is drunk?"

"Are you Lajos Kocsis?"

"Yes."

"Oh, then I must be wrong. The one I'm looking for is shorter than you and heavier. Maybe younger too."

"Cukros?"

"I beg your pardon?"

"Are you looking for the Lajos Kocsis people call Cukros? He's my nephew."

"Did he happen to live in Vojvoda Šupljikac Square during the war?"

"Yes, yes, I think so. Come in."

"I don't want to intrude."

"Not at all. I'm all alone here. And bored. It's so hot this afternoon."

"Yes. Now this Kocsis you mention, this . . ."

"Cukros."

"Right. Was he married?"

"Yes, of course. Three times. His first wife was from Srem. He was in the army, in Mitrovica. Then he got mixed up with somebody else. You know how it is when you're young. But it didn't last, and they broke up."

"Any children?"

"With the first wife? I don't think so. They only had two years together, if I remember correctly."

"No, I mean any children at all. And did he spend any time in Budapest?"

"Oh, he's been everywhere. Even America."

"For how long?"

"He was there for a good ten years, I think."

"When was that?"

"I can't give you the exact date. He went as a bricklayer, but then the war broke out and he couldn't get back. His second wife was from there."

"So he wasn't here during the war."

"No, I told you. He couldn't get back. The borders were closed."

"Well, then I am wrong. He's not the Kocsis I'm looking for. Sorry to have bothered you."

"Oh, you don't need to rush off. We were having a good talk. I used to be a teacher; I'm used to talking to people. If you're interested in other Kocsises, I can tell you that our family came here from Hungary, from Hortobágy. I went to Hungary once, and while I was there I thought I'd go to our village, Korpány. My grandfather used to tell us about it. Anyway, I get there and what do I find but seven families with the name Kocsis! Let me show you the picture we took. Just one second. I live alone and things aren't as orderly as they might be."

---

"Some other time, perhaps. I have to be going. Believe me, I have to go. Goodbye."

"I'm looking for Lajos Kocsis."

"You are? What for? Who are you?"

"An old friend. Is he in?"

"So you don't know!"

"Don't know what?"

"Oh God! He's dead. Papa's dead. He died not three weeks ago. His heart. After six days in the hospital. We hoped it would help, but no. If only I'd kept him here at home . . ."

"I'm sorry. I didn't know. But maybe your father isn't the Kocsis I'm looking for. Did he spend any time in Budapest?"

"Quite a bit. My sister lives there with her husband."

"No, I mean any extended time. During the war."

"No, we spent the war in Serbia, in Kraljevo. My mother was killed in the station bombing there."

"Then he's not the one. I'm very sorry."

"I'm looking for Lajos Kocsis."

"He's not here."

"Where is he?"

"How should I know? I don't ask him where he goes."

"Are you his wife?"

"Yes."

"Did your husband ever live in Vojvoda Šupljikac Square?"

"What square?"

"Vojvoda Šupljikac. In the center of town. There was a widow living there with her lame daughter. Did your husband ever stay with them?"

"What business is it of yours? Who are you anyway? Why are you cross-examining me?"

"So it is him. Sorry, ma'am, I just needed to know if he was the Kocsis I was looking for. He moved to Budapest during the war, didn't he? And then came back. He's the one, isn't he?"

"I don't have to tell you anything. And if it's his floozy who's sent you, you can nab him whenever you like. I don't care."

"I'm not going to 'nab' him. I just wanted to know where he lives."


"See that house over there, little boy?"

"Yes."

"Well, there's a man living there whose name is Lajos Kocsis. Know who I mean?"

"What's his name again?"

"Lajos Kocsis. An old man. Know him?"

"No."

"Sure you do. You play here, don't you? The old man in that yellow house."

"Oh, him."

"There, you see? Now, where do you think he is?"

"You mean now?"

"Yes."

"Well, I don't know where he is now, but I know he went to the bar."

"What bar?"

"Two streets down, on the corner."

"You saw him go in?"

"He's there all the time. Every day."

"Show me where it is, and I'll give you money for an ice cream."

"This is it, eh? Then lean your bike against the wall and peek in and tell me if the old man's there. Don't go in; just peek through the door. Okay?"

"Okay."

"Well, is he there?"

"Yes, he is."

"Where's he sitting? Where in the room? Left? Right? Front? Back?"

"He's not sitting; he's standing."

"I see. At the bar?"

"Yes."

"Is he the only one there?"

"No, there's some others too."

"Look, give me your hand and we'll go in together. Right. Now tell me which one he is. The one with the cap on?"

"No."

"What about the one next to him? Yes, yes, he's the one. Gray hair, hunched back, faded green shirt. He's the one, isn't he?"

"Yes."

"Then let's go. I'll walk you to the corner. Here's the money I promised. But don't tell a soul. I want this to be our secret, and if you keep it, I'll come back every once in a while for a chat. And each time I'll give you money for an ice cream."

# Chapter Six

The Blam family tree can be traced back a century and a half to 1812, when a group of approximately four hundred refugees from Alsace, the survivors of a pogrom occasioned by the proclamation of the Edict of Tolerance, headed south to Switzerland. The group included a tanner by the name of Nachmia and his wife, their six children, and his wife's father. Her father and their youngest child, Noema, died of hunger and cold on the way and were buried in two neighboring ravines on two successive days. Switzerland proved inhospitable in another respect: its Calvinist pastors forbade their flocks to have dealings with the refugees or even let them into their villages. Then a landlord in the town of Turs, which had its own Jewish colony of twenty-six families, allowed the refugees to settle there, though they had to live outside its borders and pay a head tax of one thaler a year. Since the earlier Jewish settlers were not required to pay tribute, the newcomers tried to deceive the landlord by mixing with them, which led to conflicts and reprisals.

Nachmia had hoped to work at his trade, but, lacking access to running water, he was unable to do so. Consequently, as soon as he had put up a hut for his family, he and his elder son, David, who was twelve, loaded their cart—which had brought them from Alsace—with what half-decent clothes they had left plus two goat hides Nachmia had rescued from his workshop as it burned. They hitched themselves to the cart and peddled the goods in villages along the main road. Nachmia's intention was to make enough money to buy merchandise in the city and thus develop a basis for trade.

Unfortunately, the mountainous land they crossed was sparsely populated and what peasants did live there were poor, so all they got for their wares was food—cheese and smoked meat. Still, they continued on their way, until they happened upon a band of Jewish smugglers selling supplies to both French and German troops across the German-Swiss border and were able to get a good price for the food. That led father and son to alter their plans, and for the next two years they traveled back and forth between borderland and hinterland with cartloads of food and alcohol. Then, in the third year, the entire family, which had increased by one member, crossed over into Germany.

Thanks to his close ties among the smugglers there, Nachmia started working as a middleman himself, and soon he was doing well enough to build a house. But in 1815 a group of Italian mercenaries who refused to pay picked a quarrel with him, stabbed him and David to death, threw them into a pond, and made off with their wares.

After finding and burying her husband and son, Nachmia's wife, Sarah, sold their house and moved deeper into Germany for security. Her second son, Moise, worked as a hired hand and, having proved strong and industrious, was made steward by a local landlord. He took a wife, fathered a son and two daughters, married off his two sisters, found employment for his brothers on the estate, and buried his mother when her time came. But in 1848 the peasants rose up in rebellion and burned down both the mansion of the landlord (who had escaped to the town) and the house of his steward. The frenzied mob murdered Moise, raped his daughters, and tossed them all into the fire. Nor were his two brothers spared. Only his wife, Rebekka, and his son, Eleasar, who had fled to the woods during the fire, survived.

Rebekka and Eleasar found shelter with a kind miller in town, but since the riots in Baden continued, they decided to join Rebekka's brother David, who was moving with his family to the eastern part of Germany, where, rumor had it, things were calmer. But Rebekka died en route, and David and Eleasar, who found pogroms raging all over Germany, headed south to Austria and from there to Moravia and Brno, where they found a fairly large Jewish community. David set Eleasar up as an apprentice to a kosher butcher and then traveled on with his family in the direction of Galicia, never to be heard from again.

Eleasar soon learned his trade and the ritual laws that went with it, married the butcher's daughter, and took over the business when the butcher died. As a result of the law of 1879, he became the first of his line to have a surname: Blahm. He fathered three children: two sons and a daughter. His daughter married a man from the village; Blahm made the older son, Samuel, his assistant and apprenticed the younger son, Jufka, to a tailor.

After Eleasar's death, Samuel took over the business and Jufka moved north to the town of Ostrava, where, caring little for the not particularly remunerative tailor's trade, he took a lame but well-to-do bride and opened a tavern. He was soon left a widower with a son and daughter. He married the daughter to a businessman by the name of Josef Ehrlich, who took her and her dowry to Vienna to open a shop. Samuel kept his son, Jakob, at home to help him in the tavern.

Jakob grew up motherless but pampered and soon proved to be a good-for-nothing, playing cards and billiards with the customers instead of waiting on them. He married a girl from a distant Slovak village (no one in Ostrava would have him for a son-in-law) and fathered two sons, Heinrich and Wilhelm. Since Jakob led a dissolute life, his father-in-law gave him the following ultimatum: either he moved in with his in-laws and lived an honest life or his wife and sons would leave him. Jakob decided to make the move and began helping his father-in-law in the shop, but continued to gamble and carouse. He died at the age of thirty-two, falling from a bridge into a ravine while drunk.

Heinrich and Wilhelm were brought up by their widowed mother and their grandfather. Heinrich was kept at home to work in the shop, while Wilhelm was sent to the Pressburg Gymnasium. After five years Wilhelm quit school and found work on a newspaper, delivering messages at first, then canvassing for classified ads. Two years later he decided to try his luck in Budapest, attracted by the city's colorful newspapers that had come his way. He was determined to become a real newspaperman. But when Budapest proved the last place for him to realize his dream, he moved on, first to Szeged, then to Novi Sad, where he at last landed a job on a local paper. He lost it with the fall of Austria-Hungary, but soon after—thanks to his knowledge of Czech and Slovak, which contact with the local population gradually developed into Serbian—he managed to become a reporter for the new Serbian daily *Glasnik* (The Herald), which later turned into *Naše novine* (Our News). Wilhelm Blahm had become Vilim Blam.

The family into which Blanka Blam, née Levi, was born came to Novi Sad from the opposite direction, from the south, from Serbia. Her great-great-grandfather, Meir, a livestock merchant, left Smederevo in 1820 (the town was no longer safe after the Turks departed) and moved up the Danube to Petrovaradin with his wife and two sons. He failed to gain admittance to the town, and when he tried to ply his trade outside the moat surrounding it, he was informed that non-Christians were forbidden, under pain of exile, to deal in livestock. As a result, he opened a tavern in a mud hut and lent officers and their men money at interest. When the authorities learned of his usurious activities, they sent him packing and set the tavern on fire. Meir and his family headed for Erdut, but on their way they were attacked and robbed by a band of highwaymen. Meir was killed.

Meir's widow, Mariam, found shelter with the Jews of Erdut and worked as a servant in their houses. Soon after their arrival, her elder son, Gerson, set out into the world as a peddler and never returned; her younger son, Isaak, thanks to the connections of some Erdut Jews, went to work for a Novi Sad shopkeeper by the name of Adam Hirschl. Isaak took a wife in Novi Sad and brought his elderly mother to live with him. He tried to open his own shop, but the municipal authorities turned down his request, so he moved to the village of Rumenka. There his wife bore him a son and a daughter. During the Revolution of 1848 the rebels robbed him of everything he owned and the Austrian troops, called in to take revenge on the rebels, burned his house to the ground. Mariam died, and Isaak fled with his family to Kać, where he too died four years later, never having recovered from the loss.

His widow, Rava, supported herself as a greengrocer until she married off her daughter and went to live with her. Her son, Nathan, married into money and opened a tavern. Nathan had six children: two daughters and four sons. Three of the sons found employment in shops in the vicinity, and the fourth, Avram, became the municipal inspector of scales.

Avram married and fathered two children: Karl and Blanka. He wanted them to have an education, and when he learned that the Jewish community of Novi Sad was looking for a business manager, he applied for the position and accepted the offer of a monthly salary. Karl enrolled at the gymnasium but died young of tuberculosis; Blanka attended the local secular school. When Avram unexpectedly died—of tuberculosis as well—his widow, Regina, moved back to Kać, where she lived with her sister and helped run her shop. Blanka stayed on in Novi Sad with her mother's relatives. It was there that she met and married Vilim Blam.

BLAM WAKES UP.

In the final throes of his dream he is standing in front of a thick glass wall watching several figures twisting, writhing. Since the light is poor, he sees them as a blur of simplified forms, a skein of snakes crawling about with no direction or purpose. Yet he can somehow tell that they are people rather than snakes, and he senses that something terrible is going on there—pain, convulsions, death. Though horrified, he is also irresistibly drawn to the wall. He moves toward it with leaden steps, and the closer he gets, the clearer it becomes that there is in fact a tangled mass of human bodies on the floor behind it. Suddenly a figure detaches itself from the pile, rises to its knees, then to its feet, and reaches the wall at the same time as Blam. Blam stops, and the figure on the other side leans against the wall, pressing its hands and face to it. The hands squeeze out a blood-red color and gradually turn yellow; the face squashes flat, the nose broadening like a ripe fig, the mouth dividing into two leeches, the chin twisting into a pear, and finally the eyes meet the glass, two large goggle eyes whose eyeballs the pressure of the glass enlarges like water rings. The face, deformed as it is, looks familiar to Blam. He strains to connect its twisted features and faded complexion to something in his memory. His mind runs through the circle of his acquaintances and narrows until it comes to a point in the center and Blam realizes with amazement that the face is his own.

He awakes bathed in sweat, his heart pounding.

He is in his bed, which is near the window and criss-crossed by thin strips of light passing through the venetian blind to the wall, where Janja is dressing in their shimmer. He is struck simultaneously by three sensations. First, he fights the idea of waking yet welcomes it. He experiences waking as a lie, yet the dream that waking releases him from is also a lie. He is offended by the idea that one excludes the other. He still feels the horror of the dream's image: the bodies intertwined, deformed by their suffering, with his among them. The suffering is real; he feels it inside him, in his short breath, his pounding heart, his cold sweat, and he senses, he knows that this is only the aftermath of a whole dreamed life of suffering, which he no longer remembers and whose vestiges are fading, disappearing. He does not want them to disappear. If it is his life, he wants to keep it. On the other hand, his life also consists of waking in a cold sweat and watching a woman washed in light pull on her clothes and invite him into the shelter of the day.

Second, resolved as he is to take the inevitable step, Blam realizes how ill prepared he is. His heartbeat is fast and fitful, reverberating in his rib cage as in a barrel, and after every fifth or sixth beat a needlelike pain shoots through his chest. He assumes it is an echo of the fear he felt in the dream, though he has had similar pains lately even without such stimuli, walking along the street, sitting at his desk, or simply relaxing, lying on his back. Something inside him grinds to a halt or, just the opposite, starts up, an imperfection somewhere, a defect, a faulty cog on the body's wheel designed to keep things running smoothly, to maintain the balance between effort and strength. Once the balance is gone, the heart holds back, then speeds needlessly forward, leaving him either racing after it frantically or waiting, petrified, for it to catch up with him. He is convinced that his arteries are obstructed and that the fitful, uneven beating may send him into convulsions or a stroke, that he will cry out and gasp for air, but there will be no air, and he will suffocate, flailing like a cat thrown into the water with a stone around its neck. Will it happen here, now? Blam pricks up his ears, as if death might announce its arrival with a special cry or alarm. He is paralyzed by the effort to forestall it. But how? Perhaps the thing to do is ignore its presence and devote himself entirely to life, perhaps it will spare him as long as he does that. So he fills his lungs and tries to breathe evenly; he trains his eyes and ears on life, on the far end of the kitchen, and the stitch in his chest does in fact ease gradually, his heartbeat grows slower, calmer, more regular.

But what he sees against the wall across the room only brings him new anxiety. The body bending over and straightening again, tall and supple—supple after all these years—the pink, sleek, supple body is the same as the one he saw from the tram, though then it was dressed in blue, with a bony, swarthy male arm around it. A hallucination? Perhaps, but so realistic, so like the image he had of her, that the vision instantly redefined and forever sealed their relationship. Like a symbol. Or a dream. Yes, like a dream more real than reality, deeper, sharper, since it is free of the intrusions of chance in the waking state. Like the dream he has just had. He is moving among dreams, from dream to dream, and everything not a dream is an illusion.

THE BLAMS' HOUSE in Vojvoda Šupljikac Square was a modest, one-story building, a brick building, true, but with moisture stains on the walls, narrow windows that let in too little light, low, vaulted ceilings in the cellar, and a courtyard that miserly instincts had truncated to make room for a separate backyard apartment. The trapdoor leading to the cellar bent and groaned every time it was stepped on, the sun appeared over the black roof at noon only, and the privy, which stood between the front and back building, was without water.

The house had satisfied the Blams' needs as newlyweds. They decided that rather than rent uncomfortable and costly rooms they would "put their own roof over their heads," so they willingly invested the inheritance Blanka Blam had received upon the death of her mother, the widowed shopkeeper. Then, with the rise of the Novi Sad bourgeoisie—in which the Jews, with their worldwide family connections, played a leading part—the gap between what the house was and what it could be became more and more of an issue, and eventually a number of improvements were made. Vilim Blam, who assumed the role of designer, had a passion for the latest in everything, which came with his profession as journalist and with the long hours he spent at coffee houses. Blanka Blam, lacking in imagination and social contacts but hard-headed and determined, did her best to overcome all difficulties and put his ideas into practice. Blam liked nothing better of an evening than to have a cup of black coffee and a glass of red wine served in the dining room, to take out his pencil and sketch the plan of the house on the white pages of the notepad he carried in his pocket during the day for professional purposes. He would designate doors and windows with double perpendicular strokes, eliminate existing walls and draw in others, divide up or enlarge rooms, combine or separate hallways, and then, glowing with pleasure, call his wife away from the sink to have a look at his handiwork, annoyed if she, a dripping dish still in hand, failed to grasp the plan or show the proper enthusiasm. By the next morning he would forget the vision inspired by the wine and the evening hour, but she, who had only stood by with wrinkled brow, would remind him days or even weeks later of a detail that had in the meantime taken root in her mind, and ask him to call in workmen and set aside funds. Blam would put off the necessary negotiations and either forget to collect fees due him or spend them on the way home on gifts. Eventually, however, her repeated requests would bear fruit: the windows were replaced with new, larger, square ones, a glassed-in veranda sprang up in the courtyard, running water was installed to supplement the well, and—the pinnacle of modernization—a part of the unfashionably oversized pantry was turned into a bathroom.

In the back house, where tenants, the widow Erzsébet Csokonay and her crippled daughter, lived, no such changes took place, except that every summer Erzsébet Csokonay would fasten a brush to a long pole and whitewash the walls around the tiny green windows and the glass door that gave access to her kitchen and from there to the apartment's only real room. This door had once faced the back wall of her landlords' house, which had nothing but the pantry's ventilation window high under the eaves, but now it looked out on a large, modern, wider-than-high bathroom window. And from that window, every evening, the newly pubescent Miroslav Blam watched the widow at her bath.

It might be said that this festival of nudity came about quite by chance, when one night Blam went into the bathroom without turning on the light and, noticing a hazy glow coming from the courtyard, placed the bathroom stool on the toilet, climbed up on the stool, and beheld the widow bathing. But had he not been led by a vague inkling? Erzsébet Csokonay was a pale brunette who kept a kerchief tied tightly around her hair and always walked quickly and slightly bent, as if burdened by her widowed state, her poverty, and the responsibility of caring for the child she had brought into the world with a dislocated hip. Her mute resignation was visible to the growing Blam not only as she went daily through the courtyard to work (that is, to the houses of the well-to-do when extra help was needed) and back (to feed her daughter, whom she had to leave by herself) but also in the Blams' house itself, where she sometimes did the washing, helped with spring cleanings, and so on. She worked quickly and silently, almost angrily, constantly flexing her ample body, her old skirt billowing around her like a ship's sail in a tropical wind. But Blam did not focus on her female qualities until Lajos Kocsis began paying her regular visits.

Kocsis was married, and although he lived with his wife and children at the house and at the expense of his butcher father-in-law (he was unemployed), he enjoyed the luxury of having a mistress. As he made no sacrifice for his pleasure—no material sacrifice, at least, for he lacked the resources—Erzsébet Csokonay not only had to keep working, she had to work harder, because he expected her to receive him in a clean, well-heated, well-stocked home. In her landlords' house, the front house, the new situation met with unconditional condemnation. The Blams, peering out from the glassed-in veranda, where they enjoyed sitting after noonday meals or in the evenings, and seeing the short but solid, straight-backed figure of the middle-aged man in his threadbare but neatly brushed suit making his way through the courtyard to the back house, would exchange angry, ironic looks and mumble, "There he goes again!" then launch into a long discussion about the injustice of the relationship between the vain, hollow man and the helpless, lonely widow. They would never have admitted to anyone, not even to themselves, that part of their indignation stemmed from the disloyalty of their occasional servant, whom love and the sacrifices it entailed had delivered from the bonds of slavery, for Erzsébet would leave a task at the Blams' undone whenever her idle lover showed up unexpectedly at her door.

The sixteen-year-old Miroslav, however, was instinctively aware of the self-interest involved in his parents' condemnation, and in his adolescent rebellion he took the side of the lovers. He was just coming to grips with his sexuality, as yet vague and undefined, and his parents' rejection of Kocsis as a moral degenerate only served to weaken his own moral reserves. Whenever he saw Kocsis stride through the courtyard—freshly shaven, his gray-flecked hair combed back smoothly, a frayed tie forced into a knot around his ruddy bull neck—and disappear into Erzsébet Csokonay's house, Blam's mind and thoughts would fly from the textbook he so detested into the tiny, sealed-off room where everything he longed for was actually taking place. He would spend hours imagining their kissing, hugging, panting, their naked bodies arching and convulsing in shameless lust, after which the flesh-and-blood Kocsis would emerge into the courtyard—back straight, every hair in place, face and neck even ruddier than before—to be followed a few minutes later by the widow, off to pick up her crippled daughter from school or do some housework for a neighbor, a kerchief thrown over her bent head. Blam would follow her longingly with his eyes, picturing the vibrant body under the coarse fabric of her dress, and if he happened to catch her narrow-eyed glance, he felt singed.

The night he discovered the observation point at the bathroom window, his eye went straight to the windowpanes in Erzsébet Csokonay's door, which, though hung with a gathered muslin curtain, left enough room uncovered at the top to afford him an unobstructed view of the kitchen from his post on the toilet. The widow was moving about the kitchen under a light he could not see, and Blam could tell from the intense concentration behind her otherwise fitful movements that she had something specific in mind. She piled the dishes from the table on the stove, folded the tablecloth, opened and closed the sideboard, and moved the table and chairs to one side. Then she placed a large white basin in the space she had created, went over to the stove, took the lid off a pot, picked up the pot, and poured water into the basin through billowing steam. The steam rose, spread, and for a few moments the woman was invisible, but it soon dispersed, and there she was without the kerchief, her long chestnut hair pinned behind her neck. She unbuttoned her blouse, took it off, almost sloughed it off, pulled down her skirt, stepped out of it, lifted her shift over her head, and shook off her slippers. She now stood in the middle of the kitchen totally naked. Blam nearly moaned: for all his prurient conjectures he had never dreamed that the body under the coarse dress would be so tender, so beautifully put together. The widow's skin was smooth across the long milky thighs and almost transparent on the disproportionately small, quivery breasts, where it seemed to have been gathered prudishly by the two blood-red seals of the flat, finely wrinkled nipples.

Then the scene lost its titillation: the widow began to wash. She bent over, so low that her shoulders concealed her breasts, dipped a bar of soap in the basin, rubbed it in her hands, and spread the suds over her arms and shoulders, under the arms, across the chest, and all the way back to the spinal column. Then she carefully rinsed off the soap, straddled the basin, squatted, and lathered her private parts, belly, behind, and thighs. Still squatting—her breasts resting on her knees like flattened cones and her belly and private parts hidden in the shadow between her thighs, except for a tuft of short dark hair—she poured more water over herself. Then she stood up, stepped back into the basin, and lathered and rinsed her legs. She was completely visible now, glittering from the drops of water, rosy from the rubbing. She reached for a towel and wrapped it around her body, holding it at the breasts. Then she stepped into her slippers, walked through the door, and disappeared into the dark of the back room.

Frightened, Blam jerked his head away from the window and stood trembling for a few moments, wondering whether she had seen him, listening for the door to the back house to open, for the patter of slippers, for a complaint about the intruder. Nothing happened. Cautiously, still enthralled, he took another peek. It was nearly as dark outside as it was in the bathroom, and he sensed more than saw that the narrow gullet of the kitchen was now empty, the white blotch of the basin the only trace of the recent scene. Erzsébet Csokonay had most likely gone to bed.

From then on, Blam's days ended in an eagerly awaited climax. After supper, while Vilim Blam listened to the news on the radio, Blanka Blam tidied up in the dining room and kitchen, and Estera helped her mother or immersed herself in a schoolbook, he would impatiently follow the advance of the minute hand, go into the bathroom, lock the door, position the stool on the toilet, and peer out to see whether the scene of his passion and bliss had begun. There were times when Erzsébet Csokonay was so busy with housework that she started late, or when some other member of the family occupied the bathroom after supper, but Blam took all obstacles in stride, finding ever new excuses to go back to the bathroom. He could not imagine an evening without the drama of her naked body, and, although he felt frustrated, thwarted the moment the scene was over, he longed for the next.

He started missing performances when Lili appeared, filling his evenings with walks, talks, travel plans, flattering remarks about his mind and body, and in the end with the transformation of their mutual desire into physical union in the Dositej Street apartment. True, the new situation was less than perfect—there was the burden of responsibility, and there was even disappointment in some respects—but compared with the scene in Erzsébet Csokonay's kitchen it had the attraction of being tangible and fulfilling. When he stood again at the bathroom window on a free evening, he no longer felt the earlier surge of excitement. Now that he knew the secrets of a woman's body, he required more of it than the power to arouse; he required ecstasy. Then Lili left, pleading tearfully with him to follow, but war came, and the Occupation, tearing Blam away from his nebulous broodings and hurling him into the raw world of violence, mortal fear, and sudden twists of fate.

One of those twists, minor as it may have been, was that Kocsis moved in with the widow Csokonay. By then the Blams were second-class citizens and, not daring to protest, could only look on helplessly when late every morning the graying dandy, freshly combed and shaven, left the back house as if it were his own, bowing with new dignity in the direction of the veranda, where his greetings were returned with reluctant, nervous smiles. Before long he started carrying a new leather briefcase under his arm, a sign of gainful employment, which—to make matters even more humiliating—bore a certain resemblance to Vilim Blam's means of gainful employment: in tune with the upsurge in Hungarian nationalism Kocsis had been hired as a door-to-door salesman for a luxuriously appointed volume celebrating the return of Novi Sad and the entire Bačka region to the land of Saint Stephen. Only Erzsébet Csokonay was untouched by the events: she went on running from house to house to clean and waiting for her crippled child and ne'er-do-well lover to return home. Kocsis's commissions must have come in slowly, or else he used them as pocket money—in this way too coming offensively close to Vilim Blam—because Erzsébet Csokonay continued to wear the shabby dresses that concealed the splendor of her flesh.

One evening, driven almost mad by the news of executions throughout the city, Blam came home earlier than usual and, suddenly recalling her body, climbed to the bathroom window and peered into the lighted kitchen. He found it changed: there was a white bed behind the sideboard, and the widow's crippled daughter was sitting at the table, now closer to the stove, dipping her long, red pen into a square inkpot and doing her homework. Blam waited patiently but saw the widow only once, when she came into the room to turn down the sheets and help her daughter undress. Clearly she and Kocsis had the large room to themselves. Where and when did she bathe now? Blam had no idea; nor did he try to find out. The spell of those nocturnal scenes had been broken, and the new reality deprived him of the will to bring them back.

# Chapter Seven

Are you up?" the woman asks in a low voice. She must have heard Blam stirring. "It's six thirty."

It is more admonishment than statement of fact. Stocking in hand, she takes a step to the table and pushes the metal cap of the alarm clock with a pudgy index finger: no need for it to ring. Every morning after the clock does its silent job of measuring time on her side of the bed, she moves it to the table and sets the alarm that she doesn't use, not wishing to disturb the Little One's sleep.

Her effort on his behalf affords him a slight, malicious satisfaction. "Coming," he says, though he merely props himself up on his elbows. Janja has suggested they buy another clock for his bed, but he says no, claiming that the ticking bothers him. What he really wants is for her to wake him, because it makes her think of him the moment she opens her eyes.

Think of him. He knows what she thinks of him. He knows she wrinkles her prominent forehead and pictures him with his eyes on the ground, mute and motionless, an object. An object you've got to set in motion if you're going to get anything out of it. That's what he is to her.

But it doesn't matter. He's just one object among the many hemming her in. The others force her to brush against him now and then. If she had more of them, if the kitchen were smaller and crammed with things and if her bed were here too, they'd have to touch all the time. Maybe then—body to body, breath to breath—they'd feel the need to put their arms around each other on a morning like this, when the imagination is more footloose, even after insane dreams that make your heart pound—or because of them.

What he wouldn't give to pull her into bed now, to bury himself in her soft, freshly washed skin, to sink into her supple body and find freedom from his sweaty, insecure self. He feels his arms ready to reach, feels his hands and groin quivering with desire, but the request that must precede the embrace—no, he cannot bring himself to utter it; he cannot even imagine putting it into words. Words—real words, words that demand or explain—have long since died between the two of them. He rooted them out himself after catching sight of her from the tram. He made himself dumb rather than try to keep her or accept what she did. The words they exchange now are superficial, almost mocking in their matter-of-factness.

"I'm dripping with sweat," he grumbles.

Janja pauses in the minute motions that make up her dressing ritual and stands up straight, her bare arms and shoulders rosy in the light of the sun.

"Want a towel?"

He is unnerved by her naked beauty, glowing, willing to accommodate but not to love.

"Don't be silly. I'll get it myself."

He drops his feet to the rug covering the cold tiles, steps into his slippers, and squeezes through the narrow passageway between the bed and the table to the sink-and-shower combination. The kitchen-bedroom was originally a bathroom that Janja cleverly remodeled, leaving the main room for the Little One. And for herself, of course, because she is utterly devoted to the Little One.

Now each is busy in opposite corners—he washing under the tap, she finishing her dressing—their bends and arm movements all but synchronized. But it is pure habit: her thoughts are far removed from him, he knows—at the restaurant, perhaps, where a boisterous group of friends await her daily, or here with the Little One, who is still asleep.

They finish at the same time and walk over to the window together, she to raise the venetian blind and open it, he to toss his pajamas on the bed and take his shirt from the chair.

Janja picks up the pajamas from the bed, holding them as far away from her body as she can, and lays them out on the windowsill, where the sun is beating.

"So they'll dry. But shut the window when the Little One wakes up. Because of drafts."

She goes to the refrigerator, opens it, and, bending over, sticks her head into its cool light.

"Don't forget to give the Little One butter and honey. And take the chill off the milk." She issues her orders in the harsh voice of her early years. The only reason she wakes him—the only reason she acknowledges his existence—is to give orders.

"You're not going to eat anything?" he asks in turn, though he knows the answer.

"I'll have something at the restaurant."

"One of these days they'll catch you, and you'll be sorry."

"We all have breakfast there," she says, waving goodbye and flashing the usual false, bored smile.

Blam is alone. He listens to her footsteps echo through the entrance hall until they are cut off irrevocably by the click of the lock. Then he looks around. She expects him to clean up and make breakfast; he has no desire to do so. Once she is gone, he has no desire to do anything here. Everything around him looks suddenly wrong; nothing feels familiar, his own. The bed, with which they have replaced the bathtub in the alcove under the window, reminds him of a couchette in a train, and the stove, the sink, the wall cupboard, the refrigerator are so many utilitarian items, stopgaps. The distances between them were calculated to the last centimeter, as was everything else, to accommodate as many objects as possible and leave space in the Little One's room. Not that he was against it. In fact, he was the one who proposed that he move out of the main room—the child needed her peace and quiet, after all—and he had helped Janja rearrange things. It was as if he wanted to be pushed out of the family, out of their life together, to be isolated by the faceless necessities of cooking and keeping house. As if he were punishing himself for ever having tried to form a bond with, become one with, another person. Or was it that he hoped to provoke Janja into opposing him and joining him in his self-imposed exile? But she accepted his suggestions readily and without hesitation.

His heart starts up again, rasping inside his chest as though it had outgrown the rib cage. He knows this comes from the unsettling thoughts he has been having, but he is fairly sure it is not dangerous; it is dangerous only when Janja is present. Hers is the hand that can and must undo the knot of his life and death. The rest is waves and reverberations.

He goes from the appliance-filled kitchen into the entrance hall, the crossroads between the main room and the outside. Here the air is close and stifling; outside it is a brisk, sunny morning. All he has to do is open another door and walk across the terrace, and he'll be out in the wind, under a blue sky. Or even in the sky. All it would take is a leap, headfirst, that would be best, abandoned as he is. Janja would be coming out of the building about then, and he would land smack in front of her like a frog. "You forgot to kiss me!" he would say with his last breath as she bent over him, dumbstruck. Yes, he would like to shock her. Though she might simply run back upstairs to see whether the jump had woken the Little One. The Little One's head, not his bleeding one, would be the one Janja pressed to her breast.

The room he now enters is enshrouded in a darkness the consistency of india ink, so tightly are the curtains drawn. He knows his way, however, knows it almost better than he knows his way around the room he lives in: everything has its natural place, in an instinctual sort of way: wardrobes on one side, table in the middle, settees in the corner flanking the tiled stove, and plenty of space along the soft rug leading to the window. His outstretched hands soon feel their way to the cord for the roller blind, which with a creak of the slats lets a beam of light into the room.

The girl is lying with her back to the window, so Blam must go around the bed before talking to her. The pillow has cast a shadow over her face, but her healthy baby complexion shines, conquering the dark. It is oval, her face, and simple, with blond locks strewn over forehead and cheeks, the face of a young Janja, a Janja still in the making, still gentle and tender. And of whoever sired her. Popadić? Or any one of the many casual lovers Janja surely had at the time when the Little One was conceived. He never asked Janja about it; the scene he witnessed from the tram was all the proof he needed. He observes, and the child's face confirms an already firm conviction. No, there is nothing of him in those features. And this calms him. He may admire her, watching her burgeon into an individual before his eyes and with his help, but he feels no special, dangerous parental affection for her. If she were thinner, more fragile, if her hair or skin were dull like his, if she had his deep shadows or closed expression, it would upset, even pain him. He would worry about what lay buried in the lines and shadows, seek out familiar patterns in and behind them, severed, shattered connections, as on the face he saw that morning in his dream. This face does not bind him to anything. It belongs to another world, a world with other thoughts and other problems. He is glad when the child is healthy and happy, growing fast and doing well in school; he is full of compassion when she falls ill, distressed when he goes for the doctor or for medicine, sorry he can't take the pain, the fever, the fears upon himself; she is so small, so innocent, so trusting; he is absolutely certain he would give his life for her; he would give his life for Janja too, he wouldn't think twice, it would be a relief, it would make up for his lack of emotional attachment, his deficient love.

His guilt probably makes him a gentler parent than Janja with all her zeal. Leaning over the Little One, he carefully lowers his hand onto the thin arm resting on the quilt. It is so tiny, the skin so smooth and glowing, that he is loath to wake her with his sullying touch. Still, he taps her two or three times, and she stirs, stretches, opens her eyes for an instant, then shuts them again. But in that instant his face has registered, and it has comforted rather than frightened her: her lips draw into a vague, sleepy smile.

"Time to get up, darling. Mama's orders."

She stretches again and purses her lips. She and Blam

have developed a playful way of conspiring against Janja, the embodiment of rules and obligations but also of love.

"Why?"

"I think she said you've got a lot of studying to do. Is that right?"

Her eyebrows twitch just like Janja's when Janja tries to recall something. Her face is motionless for a moment, but then she opens her eyes wide and gives a serious nod.

"There, you see?" he says and, raising an index finger like a conductor's baton, gives her the signal for their ritual repetition of a sentence he once taught her in jest when she complained how strict Janja was: "Mama is always right."

They laugh.

"Good girl," he said. "Now you get dressed, and I'll go and clean up."

Back on his own turf he is somber again. How many of his comic and tragicomic quips and gestures will remain when he leaves? None: the need for them will disappear when he does. Their life will run its course without him, might even be better when Janja takes over. There will be less confusion, less uncertainty.

He hears a door creak: she's climbed out of bed and crossed the entrance hall to the toilet. Soon she'll be in to wash, and he wants to have his bed made by then so she won't be embarrassed: she's a big girl now. That problem too will disappear once he's gone: the women will have the run of the apartment; they'll move around freely, without inhibitions. There will be more space too: they'll remove his bed from under the window and put it somewhere else or sell it, and the room can go back to being a bathroom with a few kitchen utilities added. "I have a combination kitchenette and bathroom," he can hear Janja almost boasting to one of the women in the restaurant. "It used to be a studio apartment, but we did it over." She may mention that they did it while he was alive, that he gave them a hand, that it was his idea, forgetting how much he was in their way. But she may also tell the Little One that he isn't her father and so spare her the pain.

She comes in. He makes the bed while the water splashes into the sink. He feels his pajamas—they are nearly dry—and sticks them under the pillow.

"Did Mama leave me a note?"

He turns and looks at her. She is wearing a meticulously ironed pink dress; her hair is neatly combed. She has her mother's well-groomed look.

"A note?" he asks, feigning surprise. He is well aware that the two of them constantly leave each other messages about errands to be run and deadlines to be kept. "You know what your schedule is for today, don't you?"

"Yes, Papa," she says, but with a hint of disappointment in her voice.

"Put the milk on, will you?"

She complies, leaving him nothing to do and somewhat contrite: heating the milk is a task Janja always assigns to him.

"Do you feel a draft?"

"No."

Still, he shuts the window.

The girl lifts the pot from the stove in a self-assured, feminine way and sets it on the table.

"Is it warm enough?" he asks.

"Yes."

"Are you sure? Mama told me to make sure it was warm."

The girl looks up at him, wondering whether he is making fun of Mama, but in the end she decides to smile.

"Try it."

He takes her smile as a sign of complicity and smiles back.

"No, no. You're the housewife today."

She cocks her head contentedly and starts setting the table. He sits down.

"Do you like making your own breakfast?"

"I do."

"My mother used to make breakfast for me," he says didactically, ashamed of himself for including her in his family, which is most likely not hers. "My sister too. You know I had a sister, don't you? Estera. She was a little like you. I don't mean that she looked like you, but she acted like you."

"I know."

"What do you know?"

"That you had a sister and she was killed in the war."

"Yes, darling. She and my father and mother."

"And your mother's sister, Darinka."

"That's right. My mother's sister, Darinka. And many others. Thousands."

"Why did they let themselves be killed?" she asks thoughtfully, pausing with the sugar bowl in her hand and looking at him inquisitively with her curious, clear blue eyes. "I'd have tried to defend myself, I think."

"Some of them did try to defend themselves. My sister did. She shot back at her murderers. But not everybody could. It was very hard. You'll understand when you grow up."

UNLIKE THE RESTLESS and rarely cheerful Miroslav, Estera Blam was quiet, a homebody. She liked to "rest," as Blanka Blam euphemistically characterized her daughter's tendency to sit in a corner or recline in an armchair and stare at the patterned curtains or the faces of the family as they talked. It was probably because she spent so much time indoors that, even as she grew into adolescence, she remained pale and chubby. She got on well with girls her own age, with boys too, for that matter, yet she had almost no friends. When friends of her mother brought children to play with her, she was perfectly willing to let them take over her dolls and toy furniture and miniature cake tins, but she never asked to go and see them. Like a small domestic animal, she felt most comfortable in the nook where she was born, so she loved first her house and later its extension, school. She attended school with the punctuality of a pedant: she never missed a homework assignment, kept all the prescribed paraphernalia in her satchel, and was so careful with her schoolbooks that she did not even need to cover them. Vilim Blam, whose vanity led him to favor his male offspring, secretly thought his daughter simple-minded. Nor would Blanka Blam have been surprised if Estera, for all her academic zeal, had made only mediocre progress; that Blanka had not done particularly well at school herself she ascribed as much to her sex as to anything else. But such was not the case with Estera. While Miroslav with his nimble mind stood out in elementary school, slacking off later on to such an extent that they had to hire private tutors at the end of every year to get him through, Estera was at the top of her class from the start and maintained her position there unwaveringly.

She had a phenomenal memory: anything registered by her big brown eyes and fleshy ears—word, name, number—was engraved in her memory as in wax.

Helpful as it was in school and in the normal circumstances of growing up, her memory became a burden when the wave of social reckoning reached Vojvoda Šupljikac Square. Estera suddenly found herself in the position of a hen sitting on eggs that someone had maliciously sneaked into her nest. All the ominous rumors that other people clucked at and then put out of their minds as unbelievable, she registered carefully and for all time in her impartial memory bank. She ingested all the daily news, no matter how far-fetched or self-contradictory, absorbed every émigré's story, assimilated all written and oral reports of the sufferings and deaths of innocent people, and before long her round, listless, but observant eyes and sheeplike ears were taking in the chaos occurring in her immediate vicinity.

It began when Vilim Blam, being a Jew, lost his position at the newspaper for which he had worked with all his heart and soul for two decades: he was demoted from reporting to advertising. The change would not have noticeably affected conditions at home had it not noticeably affected his morale, for although he could make as much money by selling advertising as he could by writing articles, he had no desire to invest his energy in something unless he saw it the next day, as usual, in print under his name. So instead of making the rounds of the tradesmen and artisans, briefcase in hand, he would succumb to the lure of the coffee house even more than before, drinking much too much and poisoning the atmosphere with his politics. Telephone, electricity, and gas bills began piling up on the dining room sideboard, and the grocer grew more and more insistent that his account be settled.

Blanka Blam, unfamiliar with the ways of earning money because at the onset of married life her husband had laughingly refused to share any such information with her, took to seeking advice from the neighbors, and once her naive hope of finding some simple but lucrative part-time employment evaporated, she came to the conclusion that like an impoverished widow she would have to take in a tenant. At first Vilim Blam rejected the idea outright, arguing that Hitler and his ludicrous homegrown followers were on the brink of collapse, but eventually the pressure of unpaid bills forced him to yield. He did set one condition, though: they were not to take in just anybody, a student from the countryside or petty official, people his wife would find demeaning to serve; they were to find someone who could be respected by their circle as a friend of the family. It was Vilim who brought home a tenant: an unmarried newspaperman, his younger colleague, one might even say his protégé, Predrag Popadić.

Popadić was twenty-six at the time and new to journalism. He had come to it at the insistence of his father, a well-to-do landowner in the area who had grown tired of supporting his eternal student son in Belgrade and had pulled strings with the governor, who enjoyed the influential Popadić Senior's political patronage. The young man was good-looking and had a cheerful disposition; he enjoyed dressing well and was always clean and clean-shaven, thin, black mustache neatly trimmed and wavy black hair lightly pomaded. He was not much interested in journalism, or interested only insofar as it gave him an entrée to the town's high society—more precisely, to its beautiful and beautifully groomed women, on whom he constantly trained his lively, brown, doglike eyes. But when he lacked the funds for the sort of gallant rendezvous requiring flowers or a gift (and he often lacked funds, spending extravagantly when he had them), he was content with conquests of a lower order: the widow Csokonay complained to Blanka Blam that Popadić could not keep his hands off her when she cleaned his room, and he was not above bringing a somewhat tarnished specimen of female home from a coffee house, though he always did his best to slip her through the entrance hall unnoticed.

At one time a man of such loose behavior would have met with censure in a family like the Blams, but now they looked the other way. Besides, for Vilim Blam, Popadić represented a living link with the paper, with the intoxicating smell of printer's ink, the glory of boldface bylines, and whenever Vilim found him at home alone—that is, not in disreputable company—he would fairly beg him to join the family at table, where he would interrogate him about the latest goings-on, the intrigues and backbiting that every newsroom thrives on, and the true state of politics and war preparations, which newsmen gleaned from the gossip they heard and the odd communiqué they picked up at government offices. Their conversations, which lasted well into night when Popadić lacked the wherewithal to go out on the town, were of interest to other members of the family as well. Torn at the time between the nightly scenes at the bathroom window and his first encounters with Lili, Miroslav saw Popadić as the embodiment of the free, mature male, who, when he was in a good mood, would give the lad a conspiratorial poke in the ribs and show him pictures of naked women. Estera steered clear of him—his burning eyes and masculine odor, both repulsive and attractive, were not lost on her—but she would sit in her corner for hours watching him smoke, cross his legs in their dark silk socks, and stroke his mustache.

The most complex reaction to his presence, however, came from Blanka Blam. She was annoyed with him for being so free and easy, so unreliable, for making a mess of his room and dirtying it further with visits from women of ill repute, for keeping her husband from his work and her children from their studies; on the other hand, she was enthralled by him, in that he represented her first earnings and therefore a new independence. She looked after him not as a member of the family, not as a matter of course, along a well-established emotional track, but literally, strictly, as if he were a temperamental but useful machine in constant need of appraisal and adjustment. Popadić gradually became the axis not only of her monetary calculations but also of her feelings and worries. She began to think of him as her own creation, exclusively hers to direct, to return to the straight and narrow, to make better use of—but how?

Then came the painful incident with Lili. They needed a bold yet discreet gynecologist, and neither she nor Vilim Blam nor any of their law-abiding friends could come up with one. She had no choice but to turn to her tenant with his connections in the fast, fashionable, bachelor set. Popadić not only proved ready to cooperate; as it turned out, one of his closest friends was himself the sort of doctor Mrs. Blam was looking for, and Popadić immediately undertook the delicate negotiations. Since neither Vilim nor the children were to guess what was afoot, Popadić and Blanka took to whispering together. She would slip into his room the moment she heard him arrive, hoping to find out when things would be settled and how, fretting, weeping; he would comfort her. And so it happened that in those difficult, dangerous times of commotion and secrecy, Blanka Blam's femininity underwent a feverish late blossoming, which awakened Popadić's desire and led him, early one morning when the house was dark and quiet, to lure her into his room and make her, after a bit of panicky but ineffectual resistance on her part, his mistress.

The affair went on unnoticed for a month or two, until Popadić, perhaps having come into a bit of money, set out in search of new conquests and began returning home at dawn again. One night he brought a woman who, instead of disappearing in the morning, timidly stuck her head into the kitchen and asked if she couldn't make a cup of tea for herself. Startled, Blanka Blam gave her some boiling water. But when the woman began settling in and even brought over a suitcase with her things, Blanka tearfully announced to her husband that the situation was unacceptable and it was his duty as man of the house to turn the intruder out. Assuring her that Popadić would soon tire of the girl as he had of the others, Vilim Blam only poured oil on the fire. Increasingly nervous and upset, Blanka renewed her demand, but Vilim kept giving excuses. One day, after a particularly vehement argument, she flew into the tenant's room and ordered his concubine to leave the premises immediately. In the midst of the insults and screaming that followed, the woman clutched her ample bosom, rolled her eyes, and fell to the floor, her limbs twitching wildly. Popadić shouted for help, and the rest of the family, which had been following the quarrel from the dining room, came running. Together they managed to lift her onto the bed, where her round white legs, which Popadić unsuccessfully tried to cover with a blanket, continued to shake. The convulsions loosened the woman's tongue as well as her limbs, and in her delirium she revealed that the person who wanted her removed was her rival. When Vilim Blam grasped her meaning, he screamed, grabbed a pitcher of water, the first object he could find, and—aiming perhaps at Popadić, perhaps at his wife— hurled it against the glass door. The deafening crash of broken glass put an end to the scene: the woman on the bed calmed down, Vilim Blam burst into tears, and Blanka Blam threw herself on his breast and, calling over the children, who were by then also in tears, withdrew with the family to their part of the house. The children were sent to bed, and Vilim and Blanka Blam stayed up late into the night weeping and whispering more or less the same words of reproach and repentance in the dining room, as Popadić and his guest were whispering next door.

The guest left the house that night, and it was tacitly understood that Popadić would move out the moment he found another place to live. But two days later he received notification that he was to report immediately for military duty, and his only goodbye was a note asking the Blams for permission to leave his belongings—two suitcases in the corner of his room—until such time as he could arrange for someone to come for them. He was unable to do so, however, because no sooner had his unit been assembled than it was sent to Serbia. He came for the suitcases himself two months later, dark from the sun, unshaven, and wearing a suit much too big for him: he had bought it surreptitiously from an Užice coffee house owner on the day the army surrendered to avoid being taken prisoner.

In the meantime, Vojvoda Šupljikac Square had become a battlefield, the scene of the Serbian army's retreat in disarray and the entry of Hungarian occupation forces amid a barrage of artillery fire intended to kill off the leaders of the previous regime as quickly as possible. Among the hundreds of victims in this first purge was the owner of the newspaper Blam and Popadić worked for, and the offices were soon closed. This shared misfortune, together with the blood that had flowed since they last met, served to mitigate the shame between them. Blam sat Popadić down in the dining room to hear what turned out to be Popadić's none too glorious adventures as a soldier, and when evening fell and the patrol marching past reminded them of the curfew, Blam went into the kitchen, where his wife had retreated, and after a short consultation offered the homeless Popadić his old room until things calmed down. Sincerely moved, Popadić shook Blam's hand and accepted.

Vilim Blam's generosity did not go unrewarded: spurred by the loss of his job and the desire to return to his idyllic existence, Popadić tirelessly made the rounds of his acquaintances, and although he did not realize it at the time, he was simultaneously working for his landlord. He made inquiries, offered his services, carried on negotiations, and finally found his way to the newly appointed vice-governor, a Hungarian lawyer he had often played cards with and who, as luck would have it, was entrusted with the task of putting the public life of the occupied city in order. A new round of talks and deal making followed, and one day Popadić ran home from the governor's office beaming and with two pieces of news: the Serbian paper *Glasnik* would begin publication again under a new name and under his, Popadić's, editorship, and as a sign of the government's confidence in him he had been given a three-room flat in the Mercury vacated by a Yugoslav official recently packed off to Serbia. First came the congratulations, then the farewells. On her husband's orders, Blanka Blam served coffee and wine. Popadić made a solemn vow to find a place for Vilim Blam in the new setup, not on the editorial staff, of course, which would call unwanted attention to him, but in advertising, where he had been when the war broke out. Life, different as it was, could thus basically go on as before.

Everyone but Estera accepted this situation. When the

schools opened again a few days later, she attended classes as doggedly as ever but no longer touched a textbook. Instead she read tattered, greasy, illegally published political brochures and talked furtively on street corners with a group of girls whose company she now sought as much as she had avoided it before. She spent less and less time at home, but when at home she had constant visitors, mostly girls, but a boy or two as well (Čutura came two or three times; the Blams knew him as Miroslav's friend and were surprised when he asked for Estera), and they would sit and whisper, or he would give her messages to deliver, or take her to meetings. When the summer vacation came, Estera turned into a complete renegade, leaving early in the morning with her bathing suit and a cold lunch and returning at night, dirty, sunburnt, full of scratches and with a new, coarse, mocking expression on her once round, now gaunt, wolflike, raw-boned face. She ate her supper silently and voraciously, hardly hearing her mother's reproaches, and then went off to a bath and bed.

One night she failed to come home at all, and Vilim and Blanka Blam ran all over the neighborhood looking for her. They even phoned the hospital—to no avail. She showed up at the door early the next morning, just after curfew, in her summer dress and sandals, shivering and covered with mud, and when Blanka Blam began showering her with questions and threats, Estera cut her short by saying that no one was to tell she'd been away that night if they cared for their lives. Called to the rescue from his warm morning bed, Vilim Blam tried the mild tone of an older friend, but he received an even sharper response, namely, that people were different and so they should mind their own business, as she had when the two of them committed their indiscretions not so long ago.

That autumn, like most of her friends, she went back to school, but one day late in October, when her mother was expecting her home for lunch, two agents appeared at the door asking for Estera Blam. Before Blanka had time to explain that her daughter was in school, they shoved her aside, entered the house, searched every inch of it—even under the beds in Erzsébet Csokonay's apartment—and, after tearing all Estera's books off the shelves, ordered the petrified woman to notify the police the moment her daughter showed up. But she and Vilim, who came home just after the agents had left, waited in vain. They would never turn Estera over to the police, of course; they would sneak her onto the train for Budapest, where Blanka Blam had a niece. But Estera didn't come back that day or that evening or that night. She never came back.

The morning after that sleepless night, Vilim Blam went to the Mercury to see Popadić. He woke him and explained what had happened. Popadić told him to be patient and promised to find out what he could. Vilim went home to get a little sleep, but in the afternoon he was back at the newspaper office waiting for Popadić. Still no news, Popadić said with a sympathetic shake of the head. But a short time later he was on the phone telling Blam to return to the office immediately. He sat him down and solemnly, silently handed him a sheet of paper, an official press communiqué provided by the police. At noon on 23 October 1941 the Communists Estera Blam, student, aged seventeen, Jewish, and Andja Šovljanski, seamstress, aged eighteen, Serb, were killed in an armed battle with the Royal Gendarmerie while resisting arrest. They were suspected of having taken part in antistate activities: distributing pamphlets and setting fire to grain fields in the vicinity of the city.

Blam read the communiqué several times but refused to accept what it said. "That's not my Estera. That's not my Estera," he mumbled, looking up expectantly at Popadić. But Popadić stood there helpless. Then Blam rose to his feet and put down the communiqué. "I want to see her." Popadić told him it was impossible: Estera had been buried in an unmarked grave and with no witnesses. He tried to make Blam face the inevitable. It was the times, he said. No one knew what tomorrow might bring or whose actions now would prove far-sighted then. "You may be proud of her someday," he said to him confidentially, ushering him out of the office and advising him to stay at home for at least a week.

But Vilim Blam and his wife did not have time to take pride in their daughter's death, their own following three months later, nearly to the day. The only person to derive some benefit from Estera's heroism was Miroslav Blam, because Popadić now transferred his favor to him—perhaps out of guilt for having sided with the murderers.

It so happened that while Estera was undergoing transformation into a political activist, Miroslav also separated himself from the family. He suddenly married, rented a furnished room as if he had no home, and, without a thought to either his further education or employment, declared himself independent. Vilim Blam, though stricken by so unconsidered a move on the part of his pride and joy, resolved to help him. Since Miroslav would not hear of coming back home and since Vilim could not afford to support two households, Vilim quickly sold the house—with Funkenstein as the agent—and passed most of the money on to his son to cover basic needs.

Such was the precarious state of affairs at the time of Estera's death. When Vilim Blam returned to work in

Popadić's office seven days after the tragic event and, encouraged by his friend to unburden himself, mentioned how concerned he and his wife were—over and above their inconsolable grief at Estera's death—about the intolerable position their son and last hope was now in, Popadić thought a moment and said that, unlike Miroslav's worried father, he regarded Miroslav's marriage as a sign of common sense. By marrying a Christian and converting to Christianity—which he, Popadić, was willing and able to facilitate through his ties with the clergy—Miroslav would avoid being persecuted as a Jew. During the next few days, while Miroslav Blam lay with his hands under his head in his rented room waiting for Janja to come home from work, Popadić made phone calls and had a number of personal conversations on his behalf, after which he told Vilim Blam to have the boy report to his office. He ordered a taxi and took Miroslav first to the Orthodox church, where a priest in full regalia was waiting, and then to the Úti Travel Agency, where Miroslav was hired as a bookkeeper. The expedition wound up at Miroslav's temporary residence, where Popadić had a chance to observe his protégé's straitened circumstances and to meet his wife, Janja. His interest sparked by both, he obtained an apartment for the newlyweds at the Mercury and, somewhat later, a regular job for Janja at a nearby restaurant.

# Chapter Eight

There are two published records of Novi Sad under the Occupation: a book entitled *Crimes of the Occupation Forces in Vojvodina, 1941–44,* which devotes an entire chapter to Novi Sad, and the run of *Naše novine,* the daily edited by Predrag Popadić under Hungarian rule.

The book was written after the war. It is therefore based on materials found in the enemy's archives, statements made by survivors and witnesses, war criminals' confessions of the atrocities inflicted on the civilian population from the entry of Hungarian troops on 11 April 1941 to their retreat on 22 October 1944. Its pages trace how the invaders put their intentions into practice; they include directives of the High Command and Counterintelligence on the use of terror against the Slav and Jewish population, on the suppression of Communist activities in their ranks and the society at large, and accounts of the arrests, transports to camps and hard labor, and beatings and killings by which the directives were carried out. In some instances, the thread from intention to practice leads through dry reports, beginning with circular number such-and-such that provides the basis for order so-and-so and ending with the measures taken and the number of people detained, imprisoned, or liquidated. In others, an eyewitness account by an onlooker or perpetrator will paint satanic pictures drenched in blood still warm and accompanied by echoing screams. We learn, for example, the grounds for officer A. B.'s decision to sentence prisoner C. D. to "trussing," which involved counting how many minutes a person could stand on his toes while bound hand and foot before fainting, having a heart attack, or going out of his mind; we learn which agent hammered tacks under Communists' fingernails, which one mashed their testicles, which one slashed the soles of their feet, or which detachment of soldiers sent to carry out a search riddled with their bullets every member of the household from Grandma and Grandpa lying ill in their beds to toddlers wailing as they ran for cover under wardrobes and tables. In other words, sometimes it takes a bit more imagination to conjure up the crime, sometimes a bit less, but crime is always the dominant goal and theme.

The second printed source, *Naše novine*, appeared as the events took place and bears the stamp of the men who masterminded them. Although it covers almost exactly the same period—from 16 May 1941, when its first issue came out, to 6 September 1944, when it closed—it gives quite a different picture. True, it contains items that read: "E. F., a Jewish cantor from Belgrade, was tried yesterday by the Supreme District Court for crossing the border illegally . . . Once he has served his sentence, he will be sent back across the border." They give everything the semblance of legality, but fail to mention that E. F. has crossed the border between Serbia and Hungary illegally in order to escape the gas chamber and that when he is sent back across the border, he will inevitably end up in one. Moreover, these or similar stories—about the decision to check identity papers in a certain part of town or the arrest of Communist suspects or the shoot-out that resulted in the deaths of Estera Blam and Andja Šovljanski—always run side by side with other items that, taken together, are meant to provide a panorama of daily life, one in which court cases and shoot-outs and other unpleasant incidents are counterbalanced by happy occasions. "Among the first to pass the driving test given yesterday morning at the driving school was the well-known radiologist Marcela Jagić." "The choir of the Cathedral Church sang its two hundredth liturgy under the direction of Professor Milutin Ružić on Saint Nicholas's Day." "A sixty-two-year-old agricultural worker by the name of Paja Nikolić tried to kill his wife and then himself in a fit of insanity... He attacked his wife Marija for no apparent reason upon arriving home the night before last." "Pera Nikolić, cabinetmaker, hereby announces his marriage to Bojana Jovanović." "Madame Biljana, the well-known cosmetics expert, will soon begin writing a column for *Naše novine*." "Barber, 24, Eastern Orthodox, owns shop, seeks suitable marriage partner. Hairdresser preferred. Send letters to 'Barber' c/o *Naše novine*." "The Kiddie Korner: Greetings, children, to your special page! Readings for the young of every age!" "*Naše novine*'s Story of the Day: The Most Expensive Kiss." "*Naše novine*'s Latest Serialized Novel: *The Investigating Corpse*." And so on.

*Naše novine* did not come out on 21, 22, and 23 January 1942, the days of the Novi Sad raid (the general curfew prevented both reporters and typesetters from leaving their houses), but neither the next issue (25 January) nor the one that followed made any mention of the event. As if on 25 January there were not more than a thousand frozen corpses lying in the streets, as if the snow were not red from blood, the walls not splattered with brains, as if a whisper of horror were not making its way through ten thousand houses. *Naše novine* reported, on that day as on any other day, first the news from the front, then the orders of the German High Command and proceedings of the Hungarian Parliament, and finally such local items as "Express Train Traffic Halted," "Thirty-Six-Year-Old Peasant Found Frozen to Death," "New Price for Thatching," "Minus Twenty-Seven Recorded at Sunrise on Friday," followed by the children's page, the story of the day, the serialized novel, the classified ads . . .

Which of these is the true picture? Both, of course, and neither. Representing as they do the opposing viewpoints of accusation and defense, finality and continuity, the essential and the superficial, openness and secrecy, history and day-to-day existence, they are like two drawings of a countryside, one showing the mountains and rivers, the other the roads and villages. The only way to come up with even a marginally accurate landscape is to superimpose one drawing on the other.

MIROSLAV BLAM'S LOVE erupted along the border that determined his behavior in school, that is, the border between Aca Krkljuš and Ljubomir Krstić Čutura. With the Occupation, the differences between these two became even more clearly marked: freed from the restraints of the classroom, Krkljuš started a jazz band and Čutura went underground. Yet both were motivated by the same stimulus, revolt, which in those early months of the Occupation, when the shock of being uprooted from the daily routine for an unforeseeable period of time and with unforeseeable consequences was still uppermost in the minds of the entire population. Revolt for the Hungarians and Germans was a matter of taking a deep breath and seizing the unexpected opportunity to rise in the world, to become rich and famous; for the Serbs, it was a matter of feverishly sniffing the air and predicting that a regime based on murder and abuse could not last forever; and for the Jews, it was a matter of stammering about how offended and humiliated they felt. But each group pinned its desire for change on revolt, as when a ship goes down, the flailing passengers grasp at full or even capsized lifeboats.

Blam was one of the passengers. He too clung to the idea of revolt, eager and apprehensive, excited and remorseful, full of hope and the darkest foreboding. Until the Occupation, Blam was a prisoner of the house on Vojvoda Šupljikac Square—in chains but with privileges—having been charged, as the only son, with the mission of acquiring a higher education and a place in society, so he could break down the walls of alienation surrounding the family. Then suddenly he was deprived not only of the chance to pursue his education but also to make use of what education he had, thereby losing both his prisoner status and his privileges and ceasing to be anything at all. Paradoxically, however, he gained by the loss. It put him on an equal footing with others. Because now schooling, jobs, progress up the social ladder—everything he had been counted on to achieve—had for tens of thousands of others become the booty of chaos, the spoils of war, blood, despotism, and destiny. They were all of them wrenched from the comfort of their homes and tossed into the street, at the mercy of the people pursuing them, closing in on them like a pack of stray dogs around scraps of meat.

Blam too, with nothing to do, no goal in life, separated from a family racked with anxiety and desperation, attracted to everything new, excited yet frightened by it like a child by fireworks, spent all his time in the street—watching. He watched the Hungarian officers in their caps jauntily pushed back, their trim tunics and gray lace-up boots, watched them strut over soil they had conquered only with the aid of a foreign power, watched them bow to and kiss the hands of the wives of newly appointed officials, the wives of new owners of shops confiscated from Jews, and the wives of Budapest lawyers who had descended on this hotbed of lawlessness like vultures; he watched the women, some beautiful, others hideous, dressed in their best but all vulgar reflections of faded glory; he watched gendarmes in black plumed hats patrolling the streets two by two with flashing eyes and with rifles slung over their shoulders, defending the new order, the new disorder, the insanity, the disease; he watched the German soldiers as they stood guard before their barracks, arrogant under their helmets, scornfully observing the spectacle they had set in motion and were now directing; he watched the Serbs and Jews, shopkeepers, artisans, and former officials stopping to have a word with a fellow sufferer, whispering, looking both ways, shaking their heads, then parting sadly to return to their deserted rooms to wait. He watched old men and women in black who, not having grasped the change or lacking the strength to adapt to it, went with heads bent to church for consolation. And he watched young people restlessly gathering, pushing, shouting in the squares, along the promenades, bursting with anger, resistance, the desire to fight, hatred, youthful indignation at injustice, foisting pamphlets on one another, sharing news, showing off the knife or pistol handles under their clothes. He saw Čutura among them, always in a hurry but purposeful, always on the fringe of a crowd he seemed to hold together with the invisible rope of his will. He saw Krkljuš dragging his saxophone case on the way to practice or surrounded by the members of his band and whistling the latest swing or fox-trot hit they would be rehearsing the next morning. Hoping to learn how to merge with a strong, well-defined group, Blam would join sometimes one, sometimes the other.

That Krkljuš exerted the greater attraction can perhaps be attributed to a certain caution in Blam or to his lack of need to give his life direction, the same need that was to lead Estera to action. Čutura was completely absorbed in providing direction, to his own life and that of others, and Blam often wondered why Čutura had never tried to involve him in his political endeavors, though Blam was also careful not to give him the opportunity. On their walks home from school, engrossed in a discussion about a teacher, student, or class incident—in other words, in a discussion about the mechanisms of human nature and human relations—they often paused at the park fence, so intoxicated by the harmony of their thoughts that they were unwilling to let go of them, and Blam would suddenly feel that he was on the verge of paying for it all, that Čutura would ask him to deliver a secret message or at the very least confide in him the plans for a dangerous plot. Then, out of fear, he would put Čutura off with a joke or pretend to become skeptical or indifferent, thus cracking the armor tightening around him but also letting them preserve the pleasure they took in their heart-to-heart talks. After all, Čutura valued their talks as much as Blam or he would not have continued with them. The talks supplied him with themes and ideas, and while he did not draw on them directly, they helped broaden his outlook. The Occupation put an end to this formative period: it required an ironclad commitment, and Čutura was ready. The fact that the Occupation coincided with the end of school and hence the end of their walks together was merely an external confirmation of their separation. Sparks of happy recognition still flew between them later when they met in the street or at a gathering, but they no longer felt the need to exchange ideas, and by the last time they saw each other, shortly before Čutura's death, the rupture lay far in the past and was complete.

Once he was cut off from Čutura, Blam followed the inertia characteristic of his dependent nature and leaned more and more in the direction of Krkljuš and Krkljuš's circle—the friends of Krkljuš who magnanimously tolerated Blam or even valued him. Again, Blam supplied them with something they lacked, because a need for ideas is often felt by people or groups with narrow interests. During those few months Krkljuš's band—Krkljuš, Raka the roly-poly pianist, Miomir the drummer, and Jole the lively trumpeter, always in a hurry and a sweat—lived only for jazz. Jazz was their revolt, their means of fending off the senselessness around them: the curfew, the blackouts, the bayonets at the ready, the orders pasted on walls all over the city. But they liked having an outsider in their midst, someone able to point out how shortsighted or vain their enthusiasm was, if only so they could recognize it better and cultivate it further. Blam was more observer than friend, fluttering around them like a fly around a swarm of bees or a hill of ants, showing up now and then at their rehearsals in Raka's house (Raka came from a wealthy family and had a piano), smoking his first cigarettes, dropping a word of encouragement, an impression, a thought, and then leaving. Or he would stay and watch silently while they argued, gesticulating wildly, waving their instruments like sabers, each whistling and humming to demonstrate that his way of doing the previous song or the song to come was right. It was with them, yet at the same time apart from them, that Blam began showing up at the Maticki Dance School, which hired the band for a pittance every Sunday from five in the afternoon until nine in the evening.

The school was located on the outskirts of town, where Karadjordje Street ends after winding through the center, in a one-story house, not quite a peasant house, with a large annex at the far end of a courtyard. The dance teacher, Ognjen Maticki (who was absent during the Occupation, having been sent to hard labor), had torn down the walls inside the annex and turned it into two large rooms: a bright entrance hall with a brick floor and a spacious main hall with a wood floor, walled-up windows, and lamps shining at all times. Dancing was confined to the main hall, but even as the dancing went on, the young men and women ran nervously to the entrance hall and from the entrance hall into the courtyard and to the gate, gathering out in front, looking for someone, waiting for someone, deciding whether to go in or find somewhere else to go, counting up money for tickets (which were sold in the entrance hall by Maticki's mother, an elderly, swarthy woman who wore a kerchief and sat at a table covered with a white tablecloth), or simply basking in the confluence of the music within and the conversations without, the smoky air and the fresh air, the bright lights and the twilight that grew darker as the evening wore on.

It was the constant commotion, the coming and going, the pushing and pulling, the indecision and sudden decisions that attracted Blam to the school. Participating in the excitement gave him a sense of relief. He would go in, usually with the musicians, take a seat on the podium behind the old, no longer shiny piano, and watch a slender, young, closely-cropped Mrs. Maticki welcome the first dancers and guide them to the chairs along the wall. He would listen to his friends tune up, or he would make an occasional comment, a suggestion about what number to open with, and not until they began to play and the couples were swirling did he join in. He would join a group of young men watching the dancers in the middle of the hall, which Mrs. Maticki did not like and put chairs against the wall to prevent. He would make up his mind which girl to ask, whether one of the quiet ones waiting along the wall or, more likely, a girl already on the floor. Cutting in was a common, even gleeful practice, though Mrs. Maticki disapproved, because life in the Occupation was looser. As a result, he could go up to a couple and separate the girl from her partner with a slight bow and dance with her until someone else cut in, at which point he would go out into the entrance hall and buy a soft drink from a well-groomed boy in a white jacket, take a seat behind the old Mrs. Maticki's back at the cloakroom (empty because it was summer), or slip out into the courtyard when it got dark, weave his way among the couples seeking privacy—catching words of love, mockery, rejection, postponement—and out into the street, where he stood to one side, hands in pockets, as the crowd pushed past, going in and coming out, its voices blending with the music in the distance, so that he was both present and absent, aware that he could go back in and resume dancing or, just as easily, leave without anyone's noticing in the dark and the crush. He loved how impersonal it all was, how he could ignore everyone around him, how coarse and natural life was outside the city; he loved this place where he was simply accepted and he could leave at any moment, because whether he came or went had no bearing whatever on the only thing people there cared about: a good time.

How wonderfully different it was from school dances, which only students attended and where under the eyes of the teacher on duty you did only the decorous steps you had learned from the dancing instructor brought in specially by the school. Here Blam found everything healthier, more interesting. The girls—shop assistants or daughters of local farmhands—were much freer, livelier, and, yes, prettier than the skinny, boring, nunlike students in their navy-blue pleated skirts and white blouses. He felt freer to strike up acquaintances when they committed him to nothing, when they lasted only a dance, even less if someone cut in. He felt no qualms, as he did at school functions, about asking the prettiest girls to dance, and it excited him to think that they took notice of him, remembered him, looked up, eager, as he moved in their direction, and even sought him out with their eyes when he happened to be near them. He was perfectly aware that most of the girls at the dancing school had steady boyfriends they would be leaving with—to go home? to take a walk? to kiss in the nearest house entrance?—and he wished he had a girl like that, so he could be like the others and take full advantage of the evening's magic. When he noticed that one of the girls he danced with quite often—a tall blonde with a prominent forehead and an easy, open smile—changed partners from one evening to the next, he concluded that she was not attached. He went up to her one evening just before the last dance and asked if he could see her home. She said yes.

The first thing she said to him when they emerged into the dark of the street was "You know the musicians, don't you. You're always up there with them."

That gave him a chance to go into the nature of his friendship with the band and even touch on how he helped plan what they were going to play and the way they were going to play it. But Janja was more interested in their personal stories: she'd heard Krkljuš liked to drink and seen

Raka in the company of a girl with a bad reputation. Blam disabused her of a good deal. He hardly noticed when she came to an abrupt stop in front of a one-story house with peeling plaster.

"This is where I live," she said, holding out her hand. "Good night."

He almost forgot to ask whether she would be going to the dance next week.

"Of course," she said, looking at him in surprise.

He could think of nothing better in response than to give her large hand a shake full of meaning and to bow.

For the rest of the week he thought about nothing but their brief walk. He had never felt so comfortable with a girl, so uninhibited and free of the fear he would do something wrong. He attributed this to her easy manner, which he suspected came from having a certain amount (maybe a great deal) of experience, and if she was so used to being courted and to the intimacies that went with it, he wondered whether he hadn't been a bit too formal with her, whether she hadn't expected him to be more forward. But when he went over everything she'd done and said, he couldn't find the slightest hint of this, so he concluded that he had done the right thing, for the first time at least. He put all his hope on the next encounter, when he would get her to talk about more personal matters and try to kiss her, and if she let him, he'd have to find a place where they could be alone—the room on Dositej Street, for instance, if it was still available.

But at the next dance things went unexpectedly badly. Not that Janja had changed; the problem was, she was the same. She welcomed him with her open smile, and even before he could finish his playful bow, she removed her hand from her partner's shoulder and placed it on Blam's. But when a short, chubby boy with a lock of hair flopping on his forehead cut in, she did the same, beaming at the new-comer and dismissing Blam with a quick nod. She was too popular, too much in demand; too many boys made up to her and vied for her favors. The situation was perfectly clear now. Still, Blam couldn't forget the straightforward way she had talked to him, and he was certain she didn't talk to other boys that way, because he didn't talk to other girls that way. He asked her to dance the next dance with him and she agreed, but someone cut in immediately, so he tried again, this time asking first thing whether he could walk home with her.

"Not tonight," she said with a slight frown. "I am otherwise engaged." And she flashed her smile at the boy who had just come up to cut in.

Blam withdrew sullenly. He was offended less by her rejection than by the vulgar way she had put it. "I am otherwise engaged." What a stupid, tasteless, unnatural, pretentious thing to say! He decided to give her up immediately and began asking other girls to dance, girls he had found attractive in the past. But he had trouble concentrating on them. In spite of himself he kept looking for her, Janja, and when he found her, he followed her every move, trying to read her large fleshy lips and keeping track of the boys she danced with. Sometimes their eyes met, and although she never turned hers away, her expression remained unchanged, bright and friendly and blank, innocent of any message. He stopped dancing and went up onto the podium to attract her attention. He leaned over Raka's shoulder, and Raka moved his head to Blam's, his fingers still running over the keys. Blam, looking straight at Janja, told Raka about a friend of his who had seen Raka with a girl of ill repute. Janja saw Blam and returned his stare, but again without a hint of the admiration or curiosity he had expected: she had apparently lost all interest in the musicians, now knowing everything she needed to know about them. So she was shallow as well, Blam concluded, almost pleased, and sat where he was without budging until the dance was over, at which time he saw her leave with a tall pale boy he had never noticed in her presence before.

It was now clear that she was unworthy of his attachment or even attention, that he should regard her as an attractive body that he might or might not have. And since he wanted to have it, he needed to concentrate on that and only that, not on his feelings or an assessment of her personality; he needed to find another occasion to approach her and then make his move, bind her to him. But it had to be the right occasion; he would have to be patient. He knew that neither the tall pale boy nor anyone else would last. The time would come when they'd all be gone, and then whoever happened to be in the vicinity—Blam, for instance—would have his day.

Two Sundays went by. She failed to turn up at the dance on the first one, and on the second she told him she was leaving early to go to the movies.

"Who with?" he couldn't help asking.

"Oh, a group of friends," she said with a shrug and a smile, but with no invitation to join them.

The band was playing a particularly fast number, and he could feel her muscular body bouncing in his arms, but neither her bounce nor his gave him any pleasure. They looked ridiculous, he thought, hopping across the rotting, rough-hewn, barrel-resonant dance floor and arguing, practically like enemies, over a silly date.

"Can I ever go to the movies with you?"

"Of course," she said simply, as if she had expected him to ask. "Next Sunday."

"But it's so far off!" he said gruffly, though his heart was pounding, and he suddenly felt the thrill of their bodies touching again.

Janja thought for a moment, her eyebrows fluttering. "All right, then. Wednesday."

"Shall I pick you up at home?"

"No, not at home," she said, shaking her head. "On the corner."

So Wednesday it was. He took great care in choosing the film, making sure it was not something she could have seen on Sunday (he forgot to ask her what she was going to see). He decided on the film playing at the Avala, the posters promising a love story he thought likely to please a girl of her sort. He bought tickets for the last row in the balcony, traditionally occupied by lovers, and set out at six. But turning down one of the narrow streets connecting Karadjordje with Šajkaška, he panicked: he didn't know the way. He went back to Karadjordje and walked more slowly, trying to concentrate, but again he was forced to return. He started once more, but couldn't tell if he was right and couldn't ask anyone either: on their walk he had been too absorbed in what he was telling her to notice the street signs. He broke into a sweat. He went back two or three more times, turning again, then suddenly found himself just where he was supposed to be: on the corner of her street, facing the house with the peeling plaster. It was half-past six. He was on time.

She was not. He walked up and down in the stifling twilight of the late summer day, looking at the house, looking at his watch. At last the gate opened, but instead of the neatly dressed, well-groomed Janja he expected, out came a disheveled girl with dusty bare feet wearing a short dress and swinging a dented red water pail. He scarcely recognized her. She greeted him with a clatter of the pail and pattered off in the direction of a pump in the middle of the square just behind the house, her bouncing dress revealing a strong pair of thighs half tan and half white. Her appearance was such a surprise, yet so powerful and natural, that instead of going after her Blam just stood there, as if under a spell, and watched her run across the square, lean over the pump to hang the pail on the spout, pump the handle (which she did with such force that the water splashed all over the sides of the pail), then remove the pail and return, slightly lopsided and flushed from the burden, her hair in her eyes and over her cheeks, the tip of her tongue between her teeth, her every step carefully balanced. It was not until she reached the house that he ran up and offered her a hand. But she jerked away in surprise, spattering her grimy knee with water and thus making it shiny as well. "Let me go," she said, "I'll be right with you!" and disappeared behind the gate.

True to her word, she came out very soon and was all clean—with her hair smoothly combed, in a white linen dress, wearing white shoes on washed feet, handkerchief and keys in hand—as if she were going to a dance. But walking next to her, Blam could not forget the image he had just had of her. It was as though he had seen her naked or in a lewd act and could no longer appreciate her regular appearance. Or, rather, much as he admired the pert, beautiful girl at his side, from then on he saw instead the flushed and breathless little girl beneath. He yearned for that little girl, body and soul; she was the feminine ideal he had long sensed and only now saw revealed. But since she had changed back, hiding her true nature, he was unable to talk freely to her and, later, unable to go through with his plan of conquest in the dark of the last row in the balcony.

True, he took her hand from her lap as soon as the lights went out, and she let him hold it, but the hand, instead of clutching or kneading his as he had hoped, lay there dry and limp. He put his arm around her waist, and she adjusted her body to give it room. He felt how firm the waist was, a taut arc between the rounded, softer areas above and below, but it remained stiff to his touch. She followed the images on the screen with rapt attention; he could see her moist eyes shining in the dark. What was she thinking? Could she sense the hunger in his fingers? He put his hand on her face and turned it to his; he put his lips on hers and pressed them. She offered no resistance and even opened her mouth obediently to receive his tongue, but she kept her eyes open and slightly to one side so as not to miss entirely the flickering images. And he had to accept it, because she accepted everything, clearly regarding it all as the duty of a girl who goes out with a boy. He kissed her again later, and after the film, and on the way home, and on the corner where he had waited for her. But there she pulled away from his embrace, saying she had to get to bed, she had to be up early, she'd see him at the dance on Sunday. Her response to his protest was "It's only three days away!"

Even after he got to know her better, she remained distant. She occasionally let him see her home or take her to a film, to a café, or for a walk; she let him hold her hand and kiss her, but she was always sober, even calculating, in any case far from the image he had had of her at the pump. But the moment he left her, the moment she was gone, his disappointment would yield to the image of her warm, half-naked, flushed body, so powerful, so alive that he felt the only reason it did not materialize for him was that he had taken the wrong tack, had been overcautious, not bold enough, and he longed for their next encounter to right the wrong. He therefore kept trying to see her and refused to be put off by her stalling. He begged so hard that she eventually agreed to let him come to the house.

"All right, if it means so much to you. But I can't guarantee I'll be there."

The very next afternoon he set off for the house with the peeling plaster, excited and festive, as if having been granted admittance to a secret sanctuary. His heart pounding, he entered the spacious courtyard, where a girl in a faded dress—a dress he recognized, because it was the one Janja had been wearing when she ran for the water—was hanging out the washing. At the creak of the unoiled gate she turned to Blam the same open, curious look that Janja had, though she was much younger, still a child.

"I'm looking for Janja," he said, unable to take his eyes off the dress.

His stare did not faze her. She turned her narrow back to him and called "Danka!" into the courtyard in a loud, almost angry voice.

A young woman with a freckled face appeared in the door of the back house and looked Blam over without much interest.

"He wants Janja," the girl explained, shaking the last drops off a man's white shirt. She did not turn around.

"You know she's not here," said the young woman, as if Blam were not present. But then she looked at him again and said with a shrug, "You can wait if you like."

He waited in the courtyard and waited so long that the young woman finally invited him in. The house consisted of a main room and a kitchen. The earthen floor was covered with rag rugs. There was little furniture apart from a number of beds, but what little there was, though it looked rather worn, was covered with starched needlepoint hemmed in blue thread. The young woman and the girl were Janja's elder and younger sisters, the tired-looking woman sitting at the kitchen table and overseeing their labors—her narrow head propped on large bony hands crisscrossed with dark veins—Janja's mother. Janja was the only one who went to work: she was a day laborer for a local landlord. The younger sister did the housework, the elder—newly married, pregnant, and living apart with her husband—spent the whole day in her former home, joining the husband only when he came back from the factory. Neither the mother nor absent brother was gainfully employed, the former because she was ill, the latter because he was lazy.

Blam gathered this information quickly and easily during his first visit to Janja's, sitting at the kitchen table and, having asked permission, smoking one cigarette after the other while he listened to the women's conversation. It was brusque, like the first words Janja's sister had addressed to him, and in the same harsh, shrill tone, as if following a pattern that came from the mother, perhaps, or someone before her, the father, who had long since died. Where are the clothespins? Have we got enough bread for supper? Does old man Miško know that Janja is busy tomorrow? Such were their topics of conversation. But whenever Janja's name came up—they were surprised she was not home yet—they would lower their voices as a sign of respect and even a hint of fear.

Just before dark, Janja's brother, smooth-cheeked and blond, his cap pushed back as far as it would go, burst in and demanded, with no greeting and in the same harsh tone the others used, to be served his supper. He sat down, planted his elbows on the table, and began shoveling cracklings and bread into his mouth, glaring at Blam without saying a word, as if he knew what Blam had come for. Then he left.

Janja turned up very late, in the pale light of a petroleum lamp. She was pale herself, her face looking smaller than usual under the wispy bun into which she had done her hair. Dripping with sweat, barefoot, she was so exhausted that she collapsed into the first chair she came to, but held on to a basket of cherries. Blam, both embarrassed and stirred by her pitiful appearance, did not dare ask her to take the walk he had planned for them, saying instead that he had simply dropped in to say hello. "Well, you chose a bad day," she replied in a voice hoarse from exhaustion but firm. "I'm really a sight. I have to wash and then go straight to bed."

She was out the next time, too, but because someone had invited her out. A young man, naturally, but neither her mother nor her sister could tell Blam who he was, just as they would have been hard put to identify Blam, never having asked him his name or what he did in life. They seemed to accept the fact that Janja was sought after; they didn't fret over it, though they didn't rejoice either: they were simply unwilling to judge. And after several unsuccessful visits their passive attitude began to influence Blam. He too sat there judging nothing, simply waiting for Janja to appear, waiting sometimes in vain, sometimes even taking a certain pleasure in the situation: it gave him the right to come back the next day, and in any case he had spent the time in her aura and shared the humility of her dear ones like a prayer.

He thus became her shadow, and though perfectly aware of this, he felt no shame. Or, at least, any shame he might have felt on Janja's account was so pervasive that it merged, as a river merges with the sea, with his original shame, the one that had sent him on a pilgrimage into the streets and among the poor on the outskirts of town. The reasons for that shame were now mercifully far from him: the house on Vojvoda Šupljikac Square, Father and Mother, Erzsébet Csokonay and Kocsis, and the secret, interconnected relations, and his own complex and impure relations, which he could not cast off because they were in his blood, his every move, his every word. And now, rising above the morass of his life, Janja. Janja, shame clarified and justified by love. Janja and her vulgarity, her moods, her caprices. Janja and her arbitrary way of holding him at bay or giving in. Janja in her innocence and shamelessness. Janja barefoot and disheveled, rosy and breathless, in her younger sister's short dress. Janja tired from work: pale, cold, and angry. Janja and her hard job, Janja and her bread and cherries, Janja and her pleasures, the dissipation and disorder all around her. He sensed more in all this than the expression of a personality or series of personalities; he sensed something primordial, indestructible, a rootedness in the soil, the soil of the dusty outskirts of Novi Sad, in the language, in the customs, which were more diffuse yet stronger than his, untouched by foreign models and influences, unconcerned with fitting in or assimilating, on the contrary, opposed to everything on the outside, opposed not by desire or intention, which is in itself a concession, but by instinct, because nothing could be more natural, because like the soil, like the language, those customs are born of instinct, the instinct for food, love, hate, for life without premeditation.

By now he did not even dare dream he could win her over, have her; the best he could hope for was that he would be won over by her, that she would grind him down and dissolve him in her, much as he had become an indistinguishable part of her dull but strong, unshakable existence, of the everyday round of simple movements and words and thoughts that, while routine, were the expression of a fundamental instinct.

He felt unreal—false, rehearsed, clownlike—when he came up with the words to ask Janja to marry him. Yet he was shrewd enough to know that she could not turn him down: compared with her, he was rich, educated, refined, he had "class," as her family put it. He also knew how much he was deceiving them with his superiority, aware of the insecurity and cowardice that lay behind it, aware how immature he was, how cowed by day-to-day existence. He knew she deserved better and would get better from any of her clumsy dancing partners or admirers, and he knew that basically he was out to use her, to squeeze what he could from her, that he was after lifeblood, ties, identity. But she was his only chance, his only love, and he reached out to her with his eyes half closed, as one plucks a flower from the rim of an abyss.

# Chapter Nine

The dulag (*Durchgangslager*, transition camp) for Jewish deportees from Novi Sad and vicinity was housed in the Novi Sad synagogue. The Hungarian authorities did not give much thought to the choice. The synagogue was a huge building designed to accommodate the entire congregation, and now it had to accommodate the flock driven in from the countryside as well, but since that flock, like its Novi Sad counterpart, had been halved as a result of hard labor for the young and a number of raids and arrests, there proved to be room enough.

The deportees entered through the gate in the iron fence, which was otherwise kept locked and under guard, in the order in which they arrived. They were then led into the sanctuary proper, where they found places for themselves and their belongings on the hard wooden benches or, once the benches were full, on the stone floor. It was late April, 1944, the weather springlike and mild. Jews were still wearing their most durable clothes and carrying carefully selected, high-calorie food in their knapsacks and bags. They were supplied with water for drinking and washing by the kitchen personnel or could drink and wash when the guards took them to the lavatory, so during the three days and three nights of their stay in the synagogue, before they were herded to the station and loaded into the train for Auschwitz, their most essential needs were taken care of. All of them, prisoners and guards alike, had long known the Jews would be deported, so these three days, the Jews' last on the soil that they had accepted as their own and that had accepted them, served both groups as a kind of breathing space, a space filled with thoughts of foreboding for the prisoners and thoughts of relief for the guards, yet its temporariness united them and made them almost friendly in their shared respect for the rules and regulations involved. The Jews sat patiently within the confines of the synagogue; the guards did their duty meticulously, showing anger only in the street, when they had to disperse curious onlookers—one group of which included a dejected-looking Blam, exempt because of his marriage.

The only discordant note in this otherwise harmonious waiting period came from the animal world rather than the human world; it came in the form of the dogs that had trotted alongside their masters to the synagogue and that remained outside when the guards refused to let them through the gates. There were not many, five or six at most, because the owners had generally found homes for their beloved pets and guardians among non-Jewish friends, or at least had managed to hide them somewhere. But these few dogs were a disturbance, because their instinctive loyalty kept them as close as possible to the people they still thought they belonged to. They were a disturbance to the Jews, who on their way to the lavatory or for water almost had to hide, fearful they would be recognized and their dogs' loving attempts to rejoin them would force them to break yet again with a world from which they had so painfully severed all ties, and they were a disturbance to the guards, who were constantly tripping over them as they watched for an opportunity to dash inside. The guards would chase them away, yelling and cursing, even swatting at them with the butts of their rifles or kicking them; they clearly considered such work beneath them, and it infuriated them. But the dogs stubbornly held their ground, their distance from the synagogue depending on how afraid of the guards they were, some huddling against a wall, others going back and forth in front of the gate that had claimed their masters, pricking their ears and twisting their necks at every noise. By the second and third day, driven by hunger, they would wander off to the nearby marketplace or follow a string bag with the smell of meat, but the moment they had had their fill, they would trot back to the gate, heads high, and take up positions at a wall or tree.

They did see their masters again. When at dawn on the fourth day a lineup began to form in front of the synagogue, the dogs rushed up and filled Jew Street with joyous yelps and fawning whimpers. The people tried to restrain their children, who wanted to throw their arms around their beloved pets; the guards shouted, but to no avail. Shooting was out of the question—though it had been suggested—because the march to the station took in the dark to keep it from drawing attention. The only recourse was to set the lineup in motion as soon as it was ready.

The dogs had a last moment of glory while their masters were waiting at the station: they could nuzzle them and wheedle a hidden morsel. But soon they were alone on the tracks. For a while they ran after the train, but they stopped when their noses lost the familiar smells. They stared in wonder at the fields and ditches where they found themselves, their long, red tongues hanging from their mouths, and started back, one after the other, in the direction of the city.

"Look who's here!" Krkljuš calls out, pushing Blam toward the door as it opens a crack.

The door does not open wider; it pauses, almost shudders, while a pair of narrowed eyes peers out of the dark.

"Come on, let us in," Krkljuš says reproachfully, but then adds in a cheery voice, "Can't you see? It's Blam!"

The door opens, but the effect Krkljuš was hoping for when he asked Blam home is lost. He is impatient, even rough, pushing his friend into the entrance hall. "Go on in," he grumbles.

Blam plunges into the semidarkness and bows to the minute figure of Krkljuš's mother, who steps back to give him room.

"You may not remember me," he says, apologizing more for Krkljuš than for himself. "I used to visit when you lived near the park."

"You did?"

She sounds dubious.

"Of course he did," says Krkljuš, stepping forward and closing the door. "He was a school friend of ours. Of mine and Slobodan's both. We used to study together."

"So you were a friend of Slobodan's." Her voice brightens in the dark. "You're not with the courts, are you?"

"Really, Mother!" Krkljuš is annoyed. "The courts! That's not why I brought him here! Blam works at the Intercontinental." He pushes his mother aside and motions to a strip of light at the other end of the entrance hall. "Go on in."

Blam does as he is told and steps into the bright daylight of a room with little furniture—a bed, a wardrobe, a table and chairs—but full of miscellaneous objects scattered about. He sees a guitar propped in a corner.

"Sit down," Krkljuš says, offering him a chair with a

gray sweater draped over the back. "No, take your coat off first. You can put it . . ." He turns and notes with a frown that there is no place for Blam to put it. "I was in a rush this morning," he mumbles, taking Blam's wet raincoat and tossing it over the bed frame. "There," he says, turning back to Blam, satisfied.

"Did the workers ever turn up?" Krkljuš's mother asks suddenly. She is standing in the doorway.

Krkljuš says nothing for a moment, as if caught unawares. Then he rubs his haggard, blotchy face with his thumb and index finger and answers reluctantly, "Not Stevo."

"Did you send for him?"

"No. Janko was too busy."

"You could have gone yourself."

"I had customers."

She sighs. "Where's the money?"

He digs into his pocket unwillingly, almost disgustedly, and tosses a wad of crumpled thousand- and five-hundred-dinar banknotes onto the table. The wad swells, as if there were a toad inside it.

"Did the Popović woman pay up?"

"No."

Sighing another loud sigh, Mrs. Krkljuš goes over to the table, gathers the wad of banknotes with her thin fingers, and leaves the room.

Krkljuš shakes his bowed head in despair. "The damned shop."

"It's a lot of trouble?"

"Trouble? No. It's a plague, a catastrophe," he says, rolling his tormented eyes. "It's dragging me down. I can't concentrate on anything. I can't do anything of my own."

"You mean compose?" Blam asks cautiously.

"That's exactly what I mean!" says Krkljuš, moving closer to Blam and overwhelming him with the stench of alcohol. "I have all kinds of ideas, but never time to sit down and sort them out."

"Some time ago, I can't remember exactly when," says Blam, recalling only that it was a long time ago, long before the last time he saw Krkljuš, several years, in fact, "I heard a song of yours on the radio. It was sung by a woman, a local."

"Oh, it must have been 'Return to Nature.'"

Blam spreads his arms to show he is at a loss. Krkljuš goes over to the corner, picks up the guitar, presses it to his stomach, and plays a melody that soars through the air. "Is that it?"

Blam nods.

"It's one of my last pieces." He drops the guitar on a pile of crumpled clothes on a chair. The strings twang softly. "It made it to the Opatija Festival. I was with the radio at the time, and they backed me." He purses his lips.

"Why did you leave?"

"Come off it, will you? They fired me. I was one of Carević's protégés. You know Carević, don't you? You don't? Well, he's an idiot. A bureaucrat. One day I turn up at the studio slightly tipsy, and the first thing he says is, 'I'm docking you.' As if I couldn't have stayed home and called in sick. I was so mad, I got plastered the next day and kept it up, day after day, until he fired me. But he didn't last long himself. The Comrades got rid of him."

"Couldn't you go back now?"

"Now I have the shop to worry about. Mother takes care of the old man, and we'd never be able to live off my salary, so it's out of the question." He rubs his wrinkled forehead and closes his eyes for a moment. Then he looks over at Blam. "How about a drink?"

Before Blam can find an excuse to say no, Mrs. Krkljuš comes into the room, her tiny face twitching suspiciously, her eyes darting between her son and his friend, then alighting on the guitar, in the hope there is some business plot in the making. Disappointed, she settles her eyes on Blam.

"Do you live alone?"

"No. I'm married."

"Children?"

"One girl."

Mrs. Krkljuš heaves a deep sigh, as if Blam has confirmed her worst fears.

"I told my husband you're here. He wants to see you."

"Mr. Krkljuš?" Blam asks, getting to his feet.

"Wait a minute!" says Aca Krkljuš angrily, pushing Blam back into his seat and turning to his mother. "Leave us alone, will you! Blam's here to see me! Me, understand?" The blotches on his face turn redder, and a quiver runs through his hollow cheeks. "Look, bring us something to drink."

"I only have coffee," she says with tears in her eyes but does not move.

"There's no need," Blam interjects to smooth things over.

But she does not seem to have heard and leaves the room.

Krkljuš bursts into laughter, but tries to suppress it by pressing his hand to his mouth. "Wait," he says and, going over to the bed, stoops down, bends over, and comes up with a small green canvas suitcase. He opens it, shuffles impatiently through some magazines and notebooks, and pulls out a flat bottle with a yellowish liquid sloshing in it. "Have some," he says, holding it out to Blam on his knees.

"I'd rather not."

Krkljuš nods approvingly, then unscrews the tin cap, tosses his head back, and takes a few quick gulps. He exhales, lifts the bottle to his lips again, and takes one long swallow. Then he screws the cap back on and drops the bottle into the suitcase.

"Open the window, will you?" he says to Blam with a wink.

Blam goes over to the window and opens it. A few tiny raindrops graze his hand.

Krkljuš starts covering the bottle with the magazines and notebooks, but pauses. "Would you like to see some of my new things?" he asks hopefully.

"Sure. Let me have a look."

Krkljuš takes a blue, a yellow, and another blue notebook from the stack in his hand and, still kneeling, lays them out, open, on the soft quilt of the unmade bed, but they close by themselves, so he bends one back and runs a trembling middle finger over the pages filled with music.

"These are melodies. All I have to do is arrange them." He bends back the yellow notebook impatiently and taps his finger on a page where the notation is neater and in black ink. "This one I sent to Raka, and he wrote back that it was worth orchestrating."

"Where is Raka?"

"In Germany, didn't you know? Frankfurt, I think, for now. He's got his own band! You can do that in Germany. The Germans have no time to make their own music."

"You could have it played here too. With all the festivals."

"Maybe you're right. I've actually been thinking of submitting a piece to Opatija. Want to hear it?"

"Sure."

But just then the door opens, and in comes Mrs. Krkljuš with a tray. Aca shoves the suitcase under the bed and gets up, shaking his knees free of cramps. "Later," he mumbles.

"So you opened the window," Mrs. Krkljuš says in a shrill, suspicious voice, still standing in the middle of the room with her tray.

"Blam was having trouble breathing."

The woman narrows her eyes, then lifts her head and sniffs the air.

She puts the tray on the table with a caustic "Hm" and turns to Blam. "I'd let Aca go his own way if my Slobodan was still alive and there was someone else to look after the business." She sighs and makes a face. "See if it's sweet enough."

Blam picks up a cup of the steaming coffee and takes a sip. "Thank you. It's perfect." But because Mrs. Krkljuš does not move, he realizes he must drink it all in her presence. Hot as it is, he ingests the coffee in small swallows and puts the cup down.

"Now we can go and see my husband."

Blam looks over at Aca, unsure of how to respond. Aca is peering down at his as yet untouched cup, as if waiting to be left alone. Blam stands and follows Mrs. Krkljuš out of the room.

They go into the entrance hall, Blam keeping close behind the small woman because the light is so poor, but then she reaches out and opens a door, and suddenly everything is light again.

They go into the room. It is larger than Aca's or looks larger because it is less disorderly. It has two old beds, an armchair, and a wardrobe that doubles as a kind of room divider. A door frame shows just above it.

Old Mr. Krkljuš is sitting in the armchair. He is wearing a pair of pajamas with a sweater pulled over them. He seems to have put on weight since the last time Blam saw him (and until two years ago he saw him often in the doorway of the shop: tall and with a protruding stomach, but with narrow hips and shoulders), and his face is bloated and moist with sweat. From the waist down he is covered with a blanket that slopes off to the right.

"Hello there, son," he says in a tremulous, gentle voice by way of greeting. "You can sit here." He motions to the bed next to him.

Blam takes a seat.

"You can smoke."

"No, thank you. I've just had a cigarette." He reaches into his pocket. "Would you like one?"

"I've given up smoking since all this began," he says sadly with a wave of the hand, then lays the hand carefully on the part of the blanket that is slipping. "Had to give up everything. But worst of all"—he leans over to Blam and waves the limp hand in the direction of the wall behind the bed—"is that Aca doesn't obey me anymore. Just drinks." He shakes his head. "And my Slobodan, my wonderful son Slobodan, is gone." His face is suddenly inches away from Blam's. "You know what happened to my Slobodan, don't you?"

"Of course," Blam says, more hastily than he would have liked, almost boastfully. To mitigate his haste, he adds, "My parents were killed in the raid too."

"They were?" says Mr. Krkljuš, coming to life. "Then we were together. I didn't know, I didn't know. Where did they die?"

"In the street, apparently, near their house." Blam justifies the vagueness of his answer by adding, "I wasn't living with them at the time."

But Mr. Krkljuš does not notice. "My Slobodan, he died in the Danube," he says, shaking his head sadly. Suddenly he looks up at Blam with renewed interest. "Are you Jewish?"

"Yes."

"Then I have something to ask you. It's been on my mind for ages. Do you know any Jewish lawyers in Novi Sad?"

"No, I don't."

"Really? Not one?"

"Not one."

"Hm." The old man huddles deeper into the armchair. "Nobody does." His face gradually resumes its defiant look. "Würzmann is no longer with us, is he?"

"No, I don't think he came back from the camp."

"That's what I heard too." His eyes seem to be pleading with Blam. "What about Vértes?"

Blam shakes his head.

"I see. Aren't there any young ones?"

"Not that I know of."

"Hm. And I gather you have nothing to do with the law."

"No. I work in a travel agency."

"I see, I see." His voice is indifferent by now. Suddenly he turns to his wife. "Isn't the water hot yet? My back is freezing!"

Mrs. Krkljuš, who has sat there listlessly until now, stands up, takes the pot off the hot plate on the bedside table with the edges of her apron, and removes the lid to let some steam escape. "Where's the hot-water bottle?"

"Here behind my back," says Mr. Krkljuš, bending forward impatiently.

Blam stands. "Let me help."

"No, no," says Mrs. Krkljuš, shaking her head. "I'm the only one who can do it." She puts the pot back on the hot-plate and turns to her husband.

"Well, I'll be going, then," says Blam. "I hope you feel better soon."

"Yes, yes," the old man responds distractedly, searching behind his back with one hand as his wife bends over him, concerned. "Goodbye. Goodbye."

Blam goes out into the entrance hall, gropes his way to the door to Aca's room, knocks, and goes in. The window is still open, and Aca is back on the unmade bed, surrounded by his notebooks, his hands between his knees, his face gloomy.

"Pestered the hell out of you, I bet," he says with a sarcastic, almost hostile grin.

"Don't be silly. We hardly talked. Well, what do you say? Are you going to play me that song?"

"Forget it," Krkljuš says with a weary wave of the hand. "Some other time. Sit down and have a drink with me."

Blam does as he is told, but as he sits, he is overwhelmed by the alcohol on his friend's breath. It is as if the bed were soaked in it. The smell makes Blam nauseated and at the same time dizzy with hunger. "You know what?" he says, aware he is about to commit a betrayal. "Let's have that drink some other time. I need to put some food in my stomach."

"All right," says Krkljuš, taking Blam's departure surprisingly well. "Time to get back to the damn shop anyway."

Blam goes into the entrance hall accompanied by his friend, who is whistling a tuneful melody.

"Say goodbye to your parents for me, will you? I don't want to barge in on them. Tell them I had to leave."

"Fine. I will," says Krkljuš and sees him down to the main entrance, where, leaning against the wall, he follows him with unsmiling eyes.

ON THE DAY she died, Estera Blam went to school as usual and spent the early morning hours in class. During the third period—mathematics with nearsighted Mrs. Bajčetić—a folded piece of paper fell onto her exercise book from behind. She opened it and read the following block-letter text: "They are coming to arrest you. Go to Mara's immediately for further instructions." It must have been smuggled in. She turned instinctively to see where it had come from, but Mrs. Bajčetić noticed a disturbance at the door and the fuss in Estera's vicinity, banged her ruler on her desk, and called the class to order. Estera hunched forward and read the message a few more times, then folded it, ripped it into tiny pieces, and dropped them into the ink bottle on her desk. Slowly, noiselessly she slipped her books into her bag, then raised her hand and asked Mrs. Bajčetić for permission to leave the room. The teacher granted it reluctantly, and Estera reached for her bag, but suddenly realized that she had no reason to take it with her, so she shoved it back into the desk and went out into the corridor. There she looked both ways, hoping to find the messenger, but seeing no one, she simply took her coat out of the cloakroom and left.

The house where Andja Šovljanski, alias Mara, lived was located on the outskirts of town, approximately a kilometer and a half from Estera's school. Estera reached it at about eleven o'clock. By that time her class and the entire school had been searched by three agents. Angry at having found nothing and having received no explanation from the school's administration or her fellow students for her disappearance, they phoned Counterintelligence from the headmistress's office and asked for additional manpower. One of the agents remained behind at the school just in case; the other two set off for Estera's house, where they hoped to find her or set an ambush for her.

In the meantime, Andja Šovljanski, Estera's comrade

from the Yugoslav Communist Youth League, had received word that her cell had been exposed and that she was to wait for Estera Blam and go with her to the village of Klisa, where the two could hide with an old woman by the name of Dara Aćimov. Andja knew the house, because she had spent the night there once after a field-burning session. The only trouble was that Andja's message had arrived early in the morning and made no reference to the fact that Estera might not receive hers until quite a bit later. Andja dressed immediately and distributed the weapons she had been given for safekeeping—three hand grenades and a small-caliber pistol—among the pockets of her winter coat. Then the feverish wait began. She was alone with her grandfather; her father, a tinsmith, was at work, she had no mother, and her brothers were married and lived away from home. After sitting for hours in her coat weighed down with weapons, she started wondering whether she wasn't wasting valuable time: maybe the instructions were wrong or she hadn't understood them correctly, or maybe something had happened since they were written, something she didn't know about, maybe more people had been arrested, Estera maybe, and here she was, sitting in a trap. By the time ten o'clock came and went, impatience got the better of discipline, and she decided to find out what was going on. She told her grandfather that she'd be back soon, that a friend might come looking for her, and that the friend should wait here for her. With that she left the house.

Estera found the door to Andja's house locked and had to knock. Andja's grandfather came to the door wearing a fur hat and a sheepskin coat and let her in when she told him who she was. They walked through the courtyard, which was bare of foliage (it was late autumn), and went into the kitchen, where a fire smoldered in the stove. Andja's grandfather said Andja would be back soon. He laid more wood on the fire and rolled a cigarette with some tobacco from a tin box, and while he smoked, coughed, spat on the floor, and rubbed the spittle into the dirt floor with the rubber sole of his shoe, Estera stood at the window in her navy-blue coat and watched for Andja.

Andja had gone to see Sofija Kerešević, the cell comrade who lived closest to her. Proceeding warily along a tree-lined path and through mostly deserted streets, she paused at the slightest noise and ducked behind a tree whenever anyone walked past, remaining there until she was certain that it was merely a local resident on a peaceful errand. At last she reached the Kerešević house, which like hers was set back from the street and fenced off. She observed it for a long time. Nothing seemed to be moving inside, but she was still extremely cautious. She went back to the corner, turned, then turned again into the street that ran parallel to the street the Kereševićs lived on. She tried several gates, and when one yielded to the pressure of her hand, she went into the courtyard. There she found an old woman tossing her chickens corn kernels from a deep white plate. She asked the woman permission to cross her garden and, without waiting for an answer, set off through the withered plants, patches of grass, and half-bare fruit trees. She recognized the Kerešević house beyond the barbed-wire fence at the back of the property. She thought she saw something black moving in the courtyard, but couldn't tell whether it was a person or an animal. She stood there, holding her breath, but when nothing seemed to move again and nothing made any noise, she slowly crawled under the fence and jumped into a ditch. The Kerešević courtyard now lay before her.

She saw no one, just the smoke coming peacefully out of the chimney in light white puffs. She straightened and climbed into the courtyard. Suddenly she caught another glimpse of the black thing. It was behind a fruit tree. She ducked just as it emerged in the shape of a human figure and started walking in her direction.

She spun around and retraced her steps, racing along the ditch and crawling back under the fence. A shout and then a shot rang out, but she did not stop. She heard a curse and saw out of the corner of her eye that the black figure was caught on the barbed wire. She ran past the startled woman with the plate of chicken feed and out into the street.

She could have kept running, out of town, through the fields, all the way to Klisa, where she would perhaps have found safety in the double attic of Grandma Dara's barn, but she suddenly remembered that her instructions were to take Estera Blam to Grandma Dara's, and she realized how wrong she had been to disobey them. So instead of running into the fields, she ran home. She heard shots, footsteps, barking, and whistling behind her, and through a fence with missing boards she saw several figures running from the neighboring street into hers, yet on she ran. When she got to her house, she slipped through the fence at a point where a board her father had not had time to reattach was lying on the ground; she even had the presence of mind to put it back so it looked as if it were firmly in place. Then she raced into the kitchen, where she found her grandfather sitting and Estera standing next to him, nervous from the echoes of the chase she had heard.

"Quick!" Andja cried and ran back out. "Let's go!"

Estera followed. They ran through Andja's garden and leaped into the neighbor's, but in front of the house they had hoped to reach they saw two gendarmes, their rifles ready. At the same time they heard the heavy pounding of a rifle butt on the door to Andja's house and the crack of wood from the blow. Another shot rang out.

About twenty steps away stood a small, neatly white-washed structure, the neighbors' summer kitchen. They made for it instinctively. Andja got there first and flung open the door. They both flew in and slammed the door shut. There was nobody inside. It was cool and quiet. Andja managed to slide the bar into the socket and bolt the door. Then she reached into her pockets, pulled out two hand grenades, and laid them on the clean empty stove.

"Take those two grenades. And make sure you don't miss."

She took the third grenade in her left hand and the pistol in her right. They then moved back to the wall and waited.

As the footsteps and whistling came closer, they could make out the voices and shouts of the men surrounding the garden. Then a shadow fell on the curtain covering the door window, and someone pressed the handle.

Andja pulled the trigger once, twice, but the gun did not fire: there were no bullets in the cartridge. She was stunned. At that moment the panes in the door window shattered, covering the kitchen floor with glass, and a rifle barrel topped by a fierce, mustached face rammed through the opening and past the curtain. The rifle went off. Andja grabbed her chest and fell to the floor with a scream. Estera jumped to the side, into the far corner, escaping the bullet intended for her. Crouching there, she realized she was still holding the grenades. She looked down at them, put them both in her left hand, and pulled the pin on one, as she had learned to do that summer in military practice.

Then she threw it at the gendarme who had tried to shoot her, but it hit the crossbar between the broken panes in the door window and fell to the kitchen floor. She leaped to her feet, pulled the pin on the other grenade and this time managed to throw it through the opening in the door. At that moment the first grenade exploded on the floor, sending pieces of metal into her head and chest and thrusting her against the wall. She too fell. Immediately thereafter the other grenade exploded outside the door, wounding two gendarmes, one in the face and shoulder, the other—the one who had shot through the window—in the stomach and leg. Then all was quiet. Not until the gendarmes from the second squad had finished breaking down the door to Andja's house and reached the summer kitchen did the shouts and curses start up again. There they found Andja and Estera lying dead on the floor, in puddles of blood slowly merging into one dark pool.

# Chapter Ten

In the *Naše novine* Christmas issue for 1941, the first year of the Occupation, the paper's cub reporter, Tihomir Savić, published a full-page feature entitled "The Life and Times of Our Editorial Board." It is written in a jocular tone, as befits both occasion and subject matter, and illustrated by five portraits (four men and one woman) from the pen of an anonymous artist with a fluent, cartoonlike hand. The article begins with a description of the office: three rooms crammed with desks and piles of newspapers, proofs, and printing plates and populated by a small army of newspapermen scribbling, dictating, talking over the phone to correspondents, assigning articles, accepting advertisements. The article goes on to introduce the members of the team separately—sketch and text, sketch and text, and so on, down the line. First comes Predrag Popadić, who is characterized as invariably well-groomed (his sketch shows him with an arrow-straight mustache over a sarcastic smile, shiny, wavy hair, and a tie perfectly tied) and coolheaded, never losing his equilibrium, not even if he is short of material for the next issue, in which case he sends a cub reporter—Tihomir Savić, say—to some "scene of the crime" or other, knowing Savić will not dare to show his face without a scoop. The subject of the second sketch, a large-nosed profile with hair sticking out behind the ear, is the chief political commentator; he is described as morose and laconic, always off in his dream world. The next, who has a round, bald head, a double chin, and two dots for a nose, is the editor for national news. He is known for injecting a note of levity into the tensions of life at the paper. Then comes a good-natured, bovine face with eyes slanting downward and a bow tie under a wiry neck. It belongs to the editor of the games and children's page, who is in fact a confirmed bachelor with no hearth or home, a connoisseur of cafés and streets after dark. The only woman—who is pictured with heart-shaped lips, long eyelashes, and a turned-up nose—is said to be not only the fastest typist in Novi Sad but also capable of brewing the most divine coffee and winding the most ornery customer around her little finger. And finally the boyish face, all eyeglasses and flowing hair, belongs to Tihomir Savić himself, who is so young that he still believes in the beauty of life: in addition to the articles that put food on his table, he writes poetry in the wee hours of the night.

Notwithstanding the superficiality of the texts and accompanying drawings, they give a recognizable if one-sided picture of their subjects, but, then, *Naše novine* looks at everything one-sidedly. The other side is lies and cover-ups, a willingness to whitewash reality—to preserve a little place sheltered from reality—with a non-existent harmony and meaning. The editors will eventually pay for that other side: the editor-in-chief, the chief political commentator, and the national news editor will be shot for collaborating with the enemy; the editor of the games and children's page will be sentenced to hard labor and die in prison; and the sweet young typist and reporter poet, who marry the following year, will escape with the retreating German troops and end up running a bed and breakfast in Australia.

Nothing Savić's article describes is left in Novi Sad today but the premises he evokes in the opening passage: the three rooms above the Avala overlooking the courtyard, then as now bustling with filmgoers before the matinees and evening shows. Immediately after the war came to an end and *Naše novine* closed up shop, the space was occupied by a young partisan officer and commissar who used it to entertain transient Comrades and local girls, but he was soon replaced by a higher ranking officer and his family. Next, the entire floor—the entire building, in fact—came under the management of the cinema, which was ordered by the local command to find the officer another apartment. From then on, *Naše novine*'s former premises resounded once more with ringing phones and clacking typewriters, though the staff was of course different: two young women—one newly married, the other, a cashier with a trace of a mustache and newly divorced—and a middle-aged family man, a former gymnast with a stiff, dignified way about him. But if a current-day reporter decided to do a feature on them, he might well come up with similar portraits; indeed, even the side of their characters omitted from the feature—their tendency to lie, though now in the more innocent guise of providing fantasies on the silver screen—could be seen as unchanged. Which confirms both the stability of the human condition and the futility of the word as a means of exposing it.

WHILE TIHOMIR SAVIĆ was hard at work on his Christmas feature, Blam spent a good deal of time just below Savić's windows in the courtyard of the Avala. These were the weeks immediately following Blam's marriage and Estera's death, a time when his summer fever of rebellious expectation, fear, and hope gave way to shock. It was in a state of shock that he made the daily but brief, tongue-tied visits to his mother and father, trying to comfort them but knowing he could be of no help, not even by reminding them of his existence as a son, a druglike substitute for the object of their attention. In addition to the state of shock, which he fought, he had a numb drunken feeling, which he embraced. He saw Estera's death—so sudden, dramatic, and out of character with the person he knew, yet so inexorably real—as the end of a period of wanderings, false hopes, and vain psychological schemes. Death was something Blam now found everywhere, in every word, movement, and newspaper report, in the patrols in the streets, the flags flying, the guards and weapons making their appearance everywhere. Anything outside those clear signs of destruction—the visits he paid to his parents, for instance—was merely an opiate, a means of putting death out of his mind for a while and thus letting it come more quickly, easily, painlessly.

The most effective opiate was his work at the travel agency: it was so hopelessly dull that during the eight hours it lasted, it precluded all thoughts of the existence of the other, absolute hopelessness. The moment he set off for home, however, the effect wore off like that of a bad medicine. At home he would find Janja waiting for him, but not the Janja of the summer vision, not Janja at the pump, hot and unkempt, who could have whipped up the frenzy he so longed for. Instead, he found the Janja he later observed from the tram, the hard and self-assured Janja who had whipped up her own frenzy with no thought of him, with her own life, her own apartment, her own job, her own lover, and everything that went with them, a Janja who, without ever having opened up to him, or softened, or brought to life the picture of her he carried with him, had taken leave of him every bit as inexorably as he had taken his leave of life.

This double image of the end proved too much for him: it drove him out of the house, into the streets, and not in search of hints or clues, as in the summer, because by now the guessing game had become a disease, a preparation for death. No, now he wandered aimlessly, looking neither left nor right, not thinking, or trying not to think, using all the strength of his legs and the warmth of his insides to push on through the cold and the sleet. He avoided human contact, especially friends, because the sight of a familiar face only called forth new visions of destruction. And yet, or perhaps as a consequence, he tended to choose the busiest parts of town for his wandering, places where people were crowds rather than individuals, impersonal, purely physical, and their moving, surging, pushing brought the fatigue he desired, like the wet snow and fierce wind. And so every day he made his way to the Avala. And one day he ran into Čutura again.

It was evening. He had just paid his visit to the house in Vojvoda Šupljikac Square, and a cold, disconsolate visit it had been, like sitting by the bed of a corpse. Yearning for contact with the crowd, he circled Main Square and had just reached the Avala and the pillars supporting the editorial offices of *Naše novine,* when he felt something brush his elbow. It was different from the listless, unconscious pressure of the crowd that kept his body steady as he made his way forward; it was a cautious yet deliberate prod. He turned, frightened. In the shadow of a pillar he made out a figure in a broad-brimmed hat and a heavy winter coat with a turned-up collar. Only the angular line of the chin, lit up by a patch of light from the lobby, told him it was Čutura.

Čutura's disguise as a vagrant or day laborer made it immediately clear to Blam that he was in hiding and that it was dangerous to be seen with him. But numbed by his solitary wandering and anxious thoughts, Blam responded to Čutura's wordless request and stopped. Čutura took a step back, to hide his face in the dark.

"I need to spend the night at your place," a tense whisper reached Blam from the darkness. "Cross the courtyard slowly. I'll follow."

Blam did as he was told. Instead of walking around the Avala's rectangular courtyard, gazing at the posters of coming attractions and immersing himself in the temporary security that they and the people who came here for pleasure afforded him, he cut through the crowd and proceeded along the narrow passage between the walls of the cinema and the courtyard apartments. The squeaky sound track of the film showing inside filtered through the bolted doors, but the passage was dark and deserted, the people in the apartments having withdrawn behind their curtains to have supper or go to bed. Not since Blam had become obsessed with death had he ventured into a place so isolated and unfamiliar, and he felt extremely uncomfortable. Stumbling on in the dark, he sensed more and more that Čutura had descended upon him when his defenses were down and was dragging him into something against his nature.

Čutura wanted to spend the night at his place. Blam could not imagine how that would work, it was impossible, and seeing how impossible it was, he saw all the more starkly the impossibility of his own situation, of his life as it was. In a series of disjointed images he pictured Čutura entering the Mercury and climbing to the mansard; he pictured himself letting Čutura in and explaining to Janja

who he was and Janja, perhaps suspicious, perhaps accepting, giving him something to eat. But through those images, he felt, more, Čutura's penetrating eyes on them,
assessing the new things Janja had brought into Blam's
life—Janja herself among them—conjecturing what their
relationship was like, sensing the discord, the division, de-
ducing from a word in passing what Janja's new job was
and perhaps even who had obtained it for her, the editor-
in-chief of the collaborationist *Naše novine* and the Blams'
former tenant. And thus Čutura would pronounce a piti-
less sentence on Blam's life. Blam did not want Čutura to
condemn his life: he wanted that life to disappear without
judges or witnesses; he wanted the shame of that life to disappear with him.

Thinking these thoughts, he reached the far end of the
Avala. Here the narrow passage broadened into a street of
sorts—one side consisting of apartments not unlike those
in the courtyard, the other of scattered hovels and ram-
shackle workshops—and the sound track, fading, was replaced by other, closer sounds: the banging of a less than
firmly closed door each time the wind blew, a child's voice
calling out. Blam stood still. What was he to do? How
could he go back on his word? He turned to survey the
passage, now as black as an abyss, and the dimly lit courtyard beyond it. Not a soul in sight. No Čutura. Had he
walked too fast despite Čutura's instructions? Yes, of
course he had; his unpleasant thoughts had driven him like
a fugitive, and he now remembered having all but run over
the uneven cobblestones in the passage. But, then, he could
indeed run, race through the next courtyard and vanish
without a trace by turning down one of the side streets. It
was an attractive possibility. He stared into the dark and
through the dark to the far-off lights, seeking the figure of

Čutura, seeking a decision, and saw that the lights did not come from the courtyard, they came from two windows above it, in other words, the windows of *Naše novine*. You could easily get there from here in the dark without anyone's seeing you, avoiding the square. Had Janja ever sneaked in like that? Maybe he'd see her instead of Čutura, see her scurrying along the passage, still flushed from her parting embrace. But no sooner did this thought flash through his mind than it was replaced by another: the thought, no, the picture of the parting embrace of Janja and Popadić, and not here but down by the customs office, a definitely more cozy and less conspicuous meeting place than the editorial offices of *Naše novine*. He could just picture it, a room in an apartment belonging to a friend of Popadić's or specially rented for the purpose, their naked bodies intertwined . . . and suddenly the image of the room with the enormous peasant bed and dark-green threadbare curtains came back to him: his own little love nest on Dositej Street.

Something moved in the darkness of the passage. It was Čutura's hat, bobbing in and out of the light behind it. Even as Blam pondered whether to wait there for him, he knew he would let Čutura down, go back on his word, but he decided for now to follow Čutura's instructions. He turned and proceeded through the courtyard, this time walking very slowly, trying to show Čutura by the sway of his gait just how slowly. At last he heard Čutura's footsteps approach and waited for Čutura to catch up with him.

For a few steps they walked wordlessly side by side, like friends accustomed to strolling together in silence. Blam could hear Čutura's breath. It sounded unnaturally loud for their slow pace.

"You go ahead when we get to the street lamps," he

whispered. "I don't want anyone to see us together. I'll follow at a distance."

Now Blam had the excuse he was looking for. He slowed down even more, hoping to give a credible imitation of surprise.

"No, that won't work," he said, carefully choosing his words to make them sound spontaneous. "I don't know if you've heard, but I live in the heart of town now." Then he added in a more positive tone, "I have a better solution. A place you can go without a chance of being seen."

"Where? Who does it belong to?"

"Nobody," he said, with an almost inaudible laugh at his own joke. "It's a sublet. For bachelors. You know, a love nest. That's what makes it unobtrusive." He was on tenterhooks. Would Čutura object?

"Is it far?" came the wheezing response.

"No, not at all. A five-minute walk."

"All right, then, take me there. But you first. The way I said."

His caution was justified, because the lights along the street were now brighter. Blam picked up speed, while Čutura maintained his slow pace and gradually fell behind, thus giving possible onlookers the impression of a man out for a stroll who just happened to be going in the same direction as the man in front of him. Only the two men knew of the invisible thread connecting them, and that knowledge, which had been such a burden to Blam back in the Avala courtyard, now brought him a certain relief. What ran through his mind now instead of nightmarish images of shame were the words and gestures he would use to ensure Čutura's safety. He knocked at the gate of the familiar Dositej Street house. When his former landlady appeared, as hunched and plodding as before but also as eager, he reminded her who he was and asked whether his former room was available, and although she shilly-shallied and pointed out that the bed was unmade and the stove unheated, she let him into the courtyard as she spoke. In the kitchen she removed his former keys from the steel key ring in the cupboard drawer and handed them to him, accepting a folded banknote in the same hand without a word. He then left, closed the door behind him, and went out into the street, where Čutura stood waiting behind the nearest tree. He showed Čutura in, locked the gate, and unlocked the door to the room at the far end of the courtyard.

When the light came on, he was doubly shocked: by the way the room looked and by the way Čutura looked. True, the room was unchanged externally—it had the same bulky bed piled high with the same bedclothes, the same bare table with rings all over the faded veneer, the same chair with the loop-shaped back and white washstand with the chipped edge, the same enamel pitcher and basin, the same green curtain over the window—but there was no frivolous, love-tryst glow to temper its shabbiness. As for Čutura, his face—the thin nose, jutting cheekbones, dry, wrinkled skin around the mouth—was emaciated, almost deformed, and his eyes revealed such exhaustion—even in the shadow of the broad-rimmed hat, that Blam grabbed the chair and moved it over to him.

"Sit down."

Čutura did not seem to hear him.

"Is this going to be all right?" Blam asked.

Čutura looked around him for the first time, and Blam, following his every movement, realized that the room was freezing and the smell of mold so strong that it was hard to breathe.

"Fine."

"Can I do anything else for you? Are you hungry? Shall I run and get you a bite to eat?"

"I don't need anything," said Čutura with a shake of the head. "Just some sleep." And slowly, sluggishly he took off his hat and laid it on the table, took off his heavy overcoat and dropped it over the back of the chair, unbuttoned his jacket, took a heavy pocket watch with no cover out of his trousers and placed it on the table. He was very deliberate, as if following a routine, but so listless as to seem absent-minded.

"Come back to the gate with me now and lock up," Blam said, "and leave the key on the table tomorrow morning when you go. Will you remember?"

"I will."

"Good. Now follow me."

He turned to go, but then, seeing that Čutura just stood there and stared after him with a glassy, distracted look, he turned back.

"Come and lock up," he said.

"Oh. Yes."

Čutura shifted his weight from one foot to the other, stretched an irresolute hand to the watch, picked it up with the tips of his fingers, and rubbed it slightly. Then, realizing the futility of what he had done, put it back on the table and turned to the door.

"Take your coat," said Blam.

Čutura obediently picked his coat up off the chair and heaved it over his shoulders as if it were a sack of grain. Then he stood still.

"Are you sure you don't need anything?" asked Blam.

"Positive. Just some sleep. You had to pay for the room, didn't you?"

"Don't be silly. Think of it as spending the night at my place."

"Right."

They plunged into the dark and made their way to the gate. Blam groped for the lock and stuck the key in.

"Lock up now. See you."

"So long."

They did not shake hands: their hands would not have found each other. Blam, having moved from the dark of the courtyard to the dark of the street, waited only long enough to hear the gate pulled to and the creak of the key in the lock. Moving blindly down Dositej Street, he recalled his last impression of light: the round glass face of Čutura's pocket watch lying on the table among the pale rings. He had never seen Čutura with the strange, old-fashioned watch before, and although he had wondered how Čutura came by it the moment he set eyes on it, he had missed the chance to ask.

AT ALMOST THE same spot where he last met Čutura—in front of the Avala and opposite the windows of the Borac Restaurant, which is on the other side of Main Square—and at almost the same early evening hour (though it was September then and the weather was milder and the war was over), Miroslav Blam stands waiting for Janja Blam. Not that he draws any parallels with that encounter or with any of the numerous others he has had here since childhood either as a filmgoer or as a passerby stopping to look at the various posters or the bustle of the crowd, though his impatient eyes do fall on the pictures of the current attraction, skim over potential filmgoers milling in the street, and dart into the lobby, of which and beyond which he knows every inch. Blam's eyes are now a decade and a half older than they were in the Čutura days, nor is his power of concentration what it was—nothing serious, of course, though basic facts from the past have been forced into deeper layers of his mind. They are still alive there and ready—should they be stimulated by, say, the chance similarity of a passerby to Čutura or Popadić or Vilim Blam—to rise to the surface and take part in the present. But as nothing of the sort occurs this time, they simply stir mutely within him like a mist.

Blam is plagued by this vague feeling whenever he waits for Janja, either at home after work or, as now, by arrangement, that is, in situations involving a deadline. He is not sure she is going to meet it, and his doubts—as his glance wanders from the Avala entrance to the windows of her restaurant—are perhaps fed by scenes of the past: Janja at the Matickis' dances, flashing an unreserved smile at all partners; Janja at the gate to her house, neat and clean and every hair in place, about to let him know that she will walk with him or go to the pictures with him (or with someone else); Janja as an invisible presence in her kitchen, in the heart of her family, which is and is not she, both familiar and distant; Janja at the pump, hot and flushed; Janja in Popadić's arms, observed from the tram, taking leave not of her lover but of him, Blam, as Blam looks on in mute admiration. All these scenes have been superseded by their life together over the years and dimmed by the years and by time's various blows and disappointments; they have been blurred by thousands of later Janjas who did his bidding or made him wait, as now, Janjas in completely different circumstances, with different looks, at different jobs. Yet something basic, the uncertainty of the promised encounter, remains flowing just beneath the dingy, listless surface of reality.

Blam thinks that the reason for his anxiety today is that he agreed to wait for Janja not far from the restaurant. From here he can be seen not only by her but also by her colleagues. They will observe him standing here like a beggar, constantly looking for her, and they will draw what conclusions they like. Even though he suspects this is not happening (Janja is too sure of herself, too vain to let her colleagues look down on him), he cannot be positive, because he is here in the street, not there, and because the curtains covering the windows are transparent only if you press your face to them. Is anyone doing that? Can anyone do that in a restaurant full of customers? Blam recalls the picture he has of the place from his rare visits: a spacious but low-ceilinged rectangle with a dozen or so tables and a door at the far end for the white blouses and aprons—Janja, a small, dark woman, the plump, middle-aged headwaiter, and, less often, the chef, with floppy jowls and a white cap, and the chef's smooth-cheeked assistant—the white blouses and aprons weighed down with plates of steaming food or congealed scraps, trays of clinking glasses or ashtrays brimming with black and white butts. "Menu, please!" "Here you are!" "Just a moment!" But he suspects that behind these orderly, almost military maneuvers a private, rebellious, pernicious life lies snakelike, barely discernible, a life of intrigues, disagreements, and thoughts never put into words yet obvious to all concerned. He suspects that behind the door that swings shut before the eyes of the customers there is a narrow passage where bodies slip by one another joking, tittering, touching hands, shoulders, and thighs, where one panting body can press against another and smell the onions and wine.

It is a life alien to him, the life of instinct, the life uncontemplated, dependent solely on the body—one's own and others'—on its movements, excretions; an ordinary life, a life beginning in the mother's womb and with mother's milk and proceeding to the first stirrings of curiosity, the first misdeeds, curses, and spankings, and on to speech and its structure beyond the meaning of words, in spite of words almost; a life free of conventions, agreements, reason, a life opposing reason, conquering it with a giggle; a life of restaurants, pubs, city streets, waiting rooms, trains, buses, and trams, but going on outside such meeting places as well, and against them, serving the carnal vices, such as drunkenness, debauchery, and hate, with the shouting and brawling born of the violence and despair that circulates in the blood. Blam wants no part of a life run by a force that cannot be controlled, predicted, or even measured, the same force that set in motion the bodies at the dance school, that gathered up the young men from the streets and armed them with leaflets and guns, that made Janja hurry back to the house from the pump with the bucket of water and choose her most attractive dress for Sunday dates, the force that once carried him along too, but only once, when he felt strong, because he believed he had the courage to perish with the pack, with the others.

Now he feels completely cut off from that force, abandoned. It has dropped him, betrayed him because he betrayed it: he only pretended he belonged to it, he never really felt at one with the city, the street, the air, the soil. He still goes through the motions, mimicking people's voices, accents, phrases, deeds, but the current that once flowed in him has long dried up: he stands alone. He stands alone in the street, surrounded by senseless commotion, shouting, signs, dazzling colors, letters, by the white of the curtains in the Borac Restaurant, curtains transparent to everyone but him and therefore concealing a secret from him, Janja's. The secret of why she rushes off every morning to her restaurant without breakfast and eats with the other waiters and waitresses, with the chef and his assistant, with the bartender and the supplier. Perhaps it is for the warmth, pleasure, distraction, easy talk, easy money, an easy way to kill time. So banal, so shallow, the allure offered by the restaurant, and he often wonders how he might win her over to some other interest. But what? Wherever he turns, he sees work, order, and reason acting as fronts for the same old profligacy, the same old vanity, the same dull gusto, pointless passion, frenzy, fuss. It withstands all rules and regulations; it comes up out of the body, out of the earth, out of an all-pervading and all-powerful desire that distorts and deforms everything; it makes Janja peer through the curtains at him standing there waiting for her while with a smothered giggle she lets a bloated hand grab her breast or dive between her legs. Yes, it is perfectly possible that that is just what she is doing while he lifts his long-suffering face to the sky to avoid staring at the opaque, motionless curtains. And then she will appear, neat, cool, and collected, running her bright eyes over him like an object, judging how usable, how useful he is to her at the moment, the way she appraises things when they go shopping together. Or will she instead rush out of the restaurant unkempt and disheveled, her cheeks bright red, her mouth half open, her eyes wild, and run breathless in the opposite direction, away from him, to another appointment, promise, folly, with her hot blood and cool love for someone else? By now Blam is almost hoping for the latter. At least he would know where he stands. Two images come together: Janja doesn't return from the pump to change for her date with him; she falls into someone else's arms and never sees him again, thereby putting an end to his suffering and confusion amid all the loose, lustful, instinct-driven bodies. He turns and leaves, goes off on his own, but where? To death, most likely, to a peace beyond understanding and confusion, beyond acceptance and rejection, where everyone is equal, no one apart and lonely, where there is no wisdom or folly, no joy or suffering.

But when the restaurant door actually opens and Janja emerges in her fitted gray coat, gray hat, and sturdy shoes, she stands at the threshold on her sturdy straight legs surveying the square until her eyes light on Blam. Then she crosses the square, her freshly made-up lips opening in a quick, confident smile.

"Waiting long?"

Blam looks up at her, suspicious, not so much of her as of himself, of his release, his excitement. It is bitter, the meaning he has found yet knows to be momentary, fleeting, on the point of melting, like a current of mild air on a cold day, into droplets of wrath and dissension.

"Oh, I don't mind. Where are we going?"

"You mean you've forgotten?" she says, staring at his face the way he knew she would, as if he were a gadget that refuses to do what it's supposed to do. "First stop is the quilt maker."

# Chapter Eleven

Look at the map of Novi Sad, and you will see a kind of spider's web intersecting on one side with a broad ribbon in the form of a half circle but extending evenly in all other directions. The ribbon, usually colored blue, is the Danube, the city's permanent eastern boundary and also its womb. For here, near its once marshy banks, the mud and fumes received the first seeds of settlement: the huts and cabins of the artisans and traders in wine and foods who from this filthy, humid lowland supplied the dry, stately military fortress of Petrovaradin, otherwise off limits to them, on the rocky shore opposite. Those early settlers brought the provisions they sold and the raw materials for their crafts from the rich hinterland plains. They built long, straight roads through those plains, roads lined with the houses of market gardeners and draymen and forming a network that grew wherever geography did not interfere. The oldest settlements, which took root along the banks between tributaries and swamps, are still designated on maps with squiggly lines that abruptly, capriciously become circles, that is, marketplaces. Today they are the business centers, the shops, restaurants, churches, and offices. They are home to the Avala and, diagonally opposite, the Mercury. The newer settlements, which sprang up along the roads, stretch deep into the hinterland and are connected by a network of transverse byways only to lose track of them and peter out finally in long, individual streets among fields, like the taut outermost strands of a spider's web invisibly attached to the center.

SUCH WAS THE map that two high-ranking Hungarian officers (a major in the gendarmerie and a colonel in the police force) had before them on the evening of 20 January 1942, as they worked out the plan for the raid they were to oversee the next morning by order of Regional Headquarters. Well-trained strategists that they were, they divided the spiderweb of the city's streets into several hundred smaller webs, assigning patrols to each from the lists of men they had been given. Each web would have a search patrol, whose job was to go through private dwellings; a roundup patrol, which was to collect all suspicious elements; and an escort patrol, which would take them to an identity check and/or execution. The task set before the two strategists was, therefore, almost abstract, consisting of a list of names and ranks, on the one hand, and a grid overlying a city, on the other. Yet behind those abstractions stood individuals with different features and different problems, and the pencil marks made by the two officers as the city was getting ready for bed determined the fate of each one of the one thousand and four hundred individuals who would perish in the course of the next three days and the fate of each of the tens of thousands of individuals who would be allowed to survive. For even though the raid had a single official goal, that of decimating the Slavic and Jewish population, and even though each patrol leader was told to be utterly ruthless, it was still up to the individual to determine, given the circumstances, the degree to which he belonged to those who were being decimated, on the one hand, and those who were doing the decimating, on the other. Or to demonstrate rather than to determine, because the degree to which each individual belonged to one or another category was largely predetermined, by birth, appearance, language, emotional and intellectual makeup, and the pencil marks of the two high-ranking officers merely combined thousands of individual characteristics into that interdependent mesh that in the next three days would—for each of them, many times over—mean life or death, sparing or killing.

THE SEARCH PATROL assigned to the Blam household was made up of two young soldiers from Hungary, two gendarmes brought in from the village of Čurug after the raid there, and Lieutenant Géczy, its twenty-eight-year-old sloping-shouldered, puffy-eyed leader. Géczy, who had been in Novi Sad since the beginning of the Occupation, had finally managed to move his young bride there until ten days before, so on the morning of the raid he arose from a warm conjugal bed. It was still dark when he slid through the icy streets in his new combat boots to the meeting place, the artillery barracks, picked up his instructions and the men detailed to him, and proceeded to the spot on the map marked in red. He was determined to be strict but fair, to accept only authentic documents, and to make thorough searches of each dwelling. By following these rules and making his charges follow them, he managed—on the first day of the raid, with only one break, at noon, when a hot meal was delivered to the men in a covered army truck—to search twenty-one dwellings along Aleksa Nenadović Street in the vicinity of Vojvoda Šupljikac Square and hand over to the roundup patrol two suspicious young men, Serbs, who had come from a nearby village to celebrate a friend's patron-saint day without proper identity papers.

"No good!" said the general with a shake of the head when he heard Géczy's report late that evening in the cold corridor of the artillery barracks, where the patrol leaders had gathered and stood in formation for an entire hour, tired, hungry, freezing, and longing to be released and find a warm spot for themselves, the lieutenant longing to be in his bed, with his wife, whose safety in these days of armed revenge gave him cause for concern. "No good at all!" And when the lieutenant tried to explain that the houses assigned to him were particularly difficult to search because they had large courtyards filled with apartments, the general turned bright red and screamed so loud that his voice echoed up and down the corridor: "I'm not talking about houses, you idiot! I'm talking about people! Criminals! Tomorrow you give me a list of a hundred criminals. A hundred, understand? How you find them I don't care! Next!"

Like the others, Géczy was not allowed to go home; he was given a bed in the barracks to share with a thickset, hairy lieutenant colonel who took off nothing but his boots, pulled virtually the whole blanket over himself, and fell to snoring immediately. Géczy could not get to sleep. His shoulders and feet were freezing. He felt like waking the large, noisy body sprawled next to him to ask how the general expected him to round up a hundred criminals in an ordinary city, though he knew perfectly well how the general expected him to do it and that do it he must. This conclusion only increased the anxiety he felt at hearing the wind howl and the snow beat against the windows and at thinking, helplessly now, of his wife alone in a strange place, with no friends, of the terrible things that could happen to her amid the general chaos.

He awoke at dawn, dazed, chilled to the bone, and angry. The lieutenant colonel and the others had all dressed. Géczy too got up, dressed, and had breakfast. He then went out into the courtyard and found his men standing in a circle and passing a canteen from hand to hand.

"What is it?" he asked the older gendarme.

"Rum, sir. They're giving it out in the kitchen. Have some."

The lieutenant was about to refuse—he thought the gendarme out of line—but the night frost, the darkness, and the difficulties of the day ahead broke down his resistance, and he took a swig from the canteen.

"We'll be doing things differently today," he said to the gendarme confidentially, feeling the alcohol taking effect.

"Whatever you say, sir," said the gendarme, clicking his heels and looking the lieutenant straight in the eye, clearly half drunk.

They set out for the house where they had left off the day before, just as the darkness began to dissipate over the ice-covered snow and a truck rumbled up to the corner and let out a roundup patrol.

"I want you to keep your mouths shut," the lieutenant said, turning to his men. "Just watch for my sign. Then out with the ones I point to."

But as luck would have it, all the houses along Aleksa Nenadović Street turned out to be inhabited by people with valid identity papers and a disproportional number of Hungarians and Germans, and whenever he tried to make insinuations about people in the neighborhood, the only response he got was a frightened "We don't know anything bad about them."

At about nine o'clock they heard a few shots, followed by a volley of fire. Géczy went out and saw that both truck and patrol had disappeared. He called over the younger gendarme—the older one's eyes were all bloodshot—and ordered him to find out where the truck had gone and where the shooting was and why, then he went on with the searches, though thinking more about the shooting, which did not let up, than about the documents and people.

"The truck's two hundred meters from here," said the gendarme, running up to him. "It's in the square around the corner. And the soldiers are doing the shooting."

"In the street?"

"Yes, in the street."

The lieutenant took the men to the next house, but what he really was concerned about was what was going on in the square. Not because he was eager to see blood but because he had a feeling that what he would see would solve his problem. And what he saw after searching the house at the very end of Aleksa Nenadović Street and turning into Vojvoda Šupljikac Square, what he saw through the bare trees of the small, snow-covered park was the large, dark shape of the truck surrounded by small, randomly placed groups of men in olive uniforms or gray civilian clothes. Shots were still being fired, loud and clear now that there was nothing to block the sound, and a chorus of wailing voices rose in response. He saw several civilians trip and fall and men in uniform bend over them, their guns spitting fire at the earth. Two contradictory thoughts flashed through the lieutenant's overwrought mind: "Everything is settled" and "Everything is lost." Then the two merged into determination and confidence.

"Follow me!" he ordered. From the first house—Vojvoda Šupljikac Square, number 11—he hauled out a young Serbian woman living in the courtyard who was unable to show how she earned her keep; from the next, a family of seven headed by a Slovak watchmaker who pleaded with him in broken Hungarian, acquired, as he kept saying, in the Austro-Hungarian army. "Take them over there, all of them," he ordered the two men he had designated as guards, pointing impatiently to the far end of the square.

His confidence reached new heights when he got to the Blams: their papers showed them to be Jews. He gave their frightened and what he judged to be cowardly faces a stern look and said, "Get your coats on!"

"But our papers are in order, sir," said Blam, playing for time.

"Silence!" Géczy shouted in the voice the general had used on him the night before. "I don't need instructions from you, understand?"

He left the two guards to watch the couple putting their coats on and took the two gendarmes with him to the widow Csokonay's. There he learned that her subtenant had a work permit but no police registration papers. He told him off—a Hungarian and failing to comply with the regulations!—then drew him aside and asked about the people in the main house. At first the man tried to wheedle out of it, but he finally gave in to the lieutenant's frown.

"You know the type. Rolling in money. Don't care much for us Hungarians. Lost their daughter not too long ago gunning down some gendarmes."

The lieutenant nodded curtly and went outside with his men. The Blams were standing in front of the glassed-in veranda wearing hats, thick winter coats, and high rubber snow boots. The soldiers guarding them had to stamp their feet to keep warm.

"That's it for here," the lieutenant called out. "Lock up the house. We can go."

He waited for the command to be carried out, then went out into the street with his two gendarmes, pausing for a moment to watch the four figures—two in formal black, two in uniform—moving across the square. He was impatient—they seemed to be moving inexcusably slowly—but at last they reached the truck and disappeared among the olive uniforms. Two shots rang out. Géczy waited for his men to emerge from the crowd, and when they saw him waiting, they started running. He made a sign for the others to follow and knocked on the door of the next house to be searched.

The house in Edouard Herriot Street, where Janja's family lived, was also in line for an identity check and search on the first day of the raid. The patrol in their part of town was led by Police Lieutenant Aladár Szalma, two well-trained policemen, and two members of the reserve forces: a shop assistant from Budapest and a strapping young peasant from northern Hungary. Szalma was a lawyer with a checkered past. Unable to find employment in his field because of the Depression, he had spent most of the thirties moving from one small town to the next as a private tutor to the children of shopowners and landowners and learning to drink on the sly and seduce the more attractive of his charges. When the borders of Hungary were expanded to include Slovakia, he began working for the police. When the borders came to include a part of Romania, he was promoted to the rank of lieutenant. Though calm and collected on the surface, he was in fact quite depraved. Still, he realized at once that the instructions "more a purge than a routine identity check" would end in a massacre, and his besotted but penetrating brain told him that he might one day be called to account for his part in it. As a result, he decided to place as great a distance as possible between himself and the dirty mission at hand and, insofar as he could, to keep his two men from it. As always when they were on a field mission, he instructed them to keep both canteens full and to take over the inspection of the citizens' documents—his eyes had a tendency to blur, he told them—though he assumed the documents would be in order. He left the searching to the older of the reservists, the Budapest shop assistant, whose overeager, doglike enthusiasm and crazed impatience for the raid to begin showed him to be mentally unbalanced. Thus Szalma devised a double plan: the identity check run by himself and having virtually no consequences and the shop assistant's hysterical search through every nook and cranny of every house and resulting in either nothing suspicious or in the discovery that under a bed or wardrobe, or in an attic behind some old furniture, there was a pistol or rifle or a whole cache of weapons. The moment the shop assistant deduced from Szalma's conspicuous laxity that all decisions about guilt would be his and his alone, he began seeing himself as a champion of the truth. Having served one master or another since his youth, he seized this long-awaited opportunity to get even with the high and mighty. He also took revenge as a spurned suitor, separating or destroying young couples still basking in the warmth of conjugal bliss or exacting their gratitude for pardoning them on account of their newlywed status, depending on whether he felt they had had enough of each other or were still desirous of pleasure and possession. And so it happened that the owners of the house where Janja's family lived, a well-to-do, flamboyantly mustached farmer and his rosy-cheeked, buxom wife—as well as the lame carpenter and his wife and child from the courtyard—were hauled off, while Janja's mother, brother, and younger sister were spared. But when the patrol reached the neighboring Margetić Street the following evening, Janja's elder sister and her twenty-year-old electrician husband were accused of harboring weapons and sent to the roundup patrol, and the roundup patrol took them to the cemetery with hundreds of others and executed them.

Karadjordje Street, which ran from the center of town to its outermost limits, was divided by the raid's strategists into two sections; the outer section, which included the house where Čutura's family lived, was assigned to Lieutenant Désberényi of the gendarmerie. Tall, dark, and handsome, a career officer and, at twenty-six, the first in his class to be promoted to the rank of lieutenant, Désberényi had had experience dealing with recalcitrant populations in both Slovakia and Romania. Moreover, he had had the luck to be assigned three gendarmes, one of whom was a sergeant and two of whom had served in the newly acquired territories for years. Only the patrol's fifth member, a corporal from the reserves, was a rookie and recently transferred to the Bačka. Désberényi immediately gave him the job of standing watch outside the houses being searched.

Realizing that he would be unable to proceed effectively without a handle on the situation, the lieutenant moved into the courtyard kitchen of a house belonging to a Hungarian and ordered the sergeant to find him an informer. The man came up with a grubby, light-haired nineteen-year-old from the neighborhood, a half German, who had been convicted several times of theft before the Occupation. Désberényi sat him down in the kitchen and gave him to understand that he was aware of his past and in the current reign of law and order he could have him put to death without anyone's being the wiser. However, he also offered the deathly pale youth the path to redemption: join the patrol and supply it with information about the inhabitants of each house before they were questioned. The young man shrugged and consented.

The first thing Désberényi learned from the sergeant when the patrol went out into the morning frost was the unpleasant fact that it was impossible to establish contact with the roundup patrol, because as the result of a foulup only one had been assigned to the entire stretch of Karadjordje Street and it had been posted closer to the center of town. He considered asking headquarters to intervene but decided against it: it would only drag things out. Instead, he would take the liquidation of suspicious elements upon himself and present the execution list to the roundup patrol after the fact, thereby giving further proof of his gift for leadership.

Off they went on their rounds. Even before entering a house, Désberényi decided the fate of its inhabitants on the basis of information provided by his informer. He left the informer outside with the corporal from the reserves—who, besides standing guard, was now required to keep the execution list—went in with his gendarmes, and read the documents, not so much to check their veracity as to confirm the identity of the condemned, whom he then handed over to the men to be shot. They reached the Krstić household on the second afternoon. Désberényi had received a particularly detailed report on the Krstić family from their young neighbor: two brothers had been taken prisoner, and another, a recent graduate, had been killed in a skirmish with gendarmes. They entered the courtyard, and Désberényi ordered the family to line up in front of the house according to age: the mother, the two daughters, and the remaining son of fourteen. He took the documents from the elder Čutura sister, set aside the mother's baptismal certificate and police registration, and read the names on the other documents aloud, waiting for each person to respond. That done, the gendarmes ordered the mother back into the house and took the three children to the far end of the courtyard. But the old woman, having heard shots all that day and the day before, guessed what was going on and instead of following orders rushed after her children. There was a scuffle, one gendarme striking her in the groin with his rifle butt, the other two hurling themselves at the children, who were trying to come to her aid. "Enough!" the lieutenant shouted and made it clear with a wave of the hand that the old woman was to be taken out with the others. One of the gendarmes picked her up, and they all walked through the courtyard to the garden fence, where the gendarmes lined them up as they had in front of the house. Then they moved back and took aim. Three shots rang out, and the boy and the younger girl fell to the ground; then another three shots, and Mrs. Krstić and her elder daughter, who had clasped her mother to her, fell together. The lieutenant went up to them and, turning all of them over on their backs with his foot, established that they were dead. Then he ordered that the bodies be taken to the gate so the roundup patrol could find them easily. He placed the old woman's documents with the rest and handed them to the reservist so he could add the names to his list.

The search patrol did not call on the Krkljuš family until the third day of the raid, a delay that saved all their lives but Slobodan's. The gendarme captain in charge was a stocky, blue-eyed, Magyarized German with a droopy red mustache. He regarded the raid as a way of settling accounts with any member of the population who was neither German nor Hungarian, because he considered the existence of such people on the territory of the newly expanded Hungarian state contrary to nature. After checking the family's papers and giving the apartment a superficial search, he ordered them to put on their coats, for "further investigation," and sent them under escort to wait at the corner, because the truck assigned to his territory was unable to take care of all his suspects, given his single, ethnic criterion and the speed of his work. When the number of suspects grew to twenty or so, two armed soldiers prodded them into action and led them through the streets on foot. On the way they passed other patrols, trucks that other frightened suspects were climbing into, and, at various crossroads, piles of corpses in the snow. After crossing the center of town and a neighborhood of newly built houses, they turned down a newly paved road that went to the public beach on the Danube. The road was dark with crowds pressed together in rows of four, guarded by soldiers on either side and facing the river, which was blocked in the distance by a row of changing cabins as white as the snow around them. Once the small column the Krkljuš family was in joined this large one, the two soldiers from the roundup patrol reported to the commander of the escort patrol and returned to the center of town.

After all the ominous scenes they had witnessed on the way, the Krkljušes were almost happy to have reached a destination, any destination, together and in one piece. Despite the guards' strict injunction against talking, they expressed their relief by asking one another whether they were cold and lamenting that they had not dressed more warmly.

Suddenly they heard shots and a burst of machine-gun fire down in front. Silence returned, but just as they began to recover, the column moved forward. When it came to a halt after ten or so steps, they strained their necks and asked the people in front what was going on. The responses were mixed, but a rumor spread through the column that, contrary to what they had been told, there was no "further investigation" at the beach, that people were being shot. Everyone was frightened. Mr. Krkljuš, gathering his courage and his knowledge of Hungarian, politely told the nearest guard that he had done an apprenticeship in Budapest and served in the Hungarian army and so was here by mistake. When ten or twelve others expressed similar concerns, the soldier, overwhelmed, stepped back, raised his gun, and threatened to fire into the column unless they shut their mouths that instant. Mrs. Krkljuš and her son Slobodan pulled Mr. Krkljuš back into the column, begging him to calm down or he would cause more harm than good. Again they heard shooting and machine-gun fire, and again the column inched forward.

The cold was now making itself felt. The soldiers stamped their feet in the snow, slapped their sides under their armpits, paced back and forth, but the people in the column could do nothing but stand or, when a gap opened up between them and the row in front, move forward. From time to time the machine gun up ahead—closer now, and clearer and louder—fired its hurried bursts, or a single shot rang out, but then whole minutes passed when only the murmur of the crowd was audible, though interrupted now and then by a child crying when its mother grew too tired to hold it and passed it on to another pair of arms. People stared at one another in horror, wondering whether what awaited them was actually possible. They could not accept it: there had to be some kind of further investigation, and they would pass muster, their documents were in order, though they were puzzled why no one seemed to be coming back from the investigation, not this way at least. Maybe some other way.

With the next round of machine-gun fire they heard—for the first time, because they were close enough now—a scream, a single scream coming from the same direction.

Their eyes filled with terror as they instinctively sought one another, joining arms, pressing closer together to fend off the shivering that came of cold and fear. Step by step they approached the entrance to the beach. Part of the column ahead of them had been checked; behind them the column kept growing, like a human conveyor belt, like grain walking to the mill.

A little girl who felt sick was taken by her mother to the side of the road to vomit, but a guard ran up immediately and chased them back. The stream from the girl's mouth spattered the shoes of the people closest to her. Then an old man lost his balance and fell facedown in the snow, his black hat rolling from his gray head. The same guard ran up and ordered him to stand, poking him with his boot. Slobodan Krkljuš bent down and slipped his hands under the man's arms to pick him up, but the guard yelled at him to get back in line. Either Slobodan did not understand or the impulse to help was too great, because he stayed with the old man, finally managing to lift him out of the snow. The soldier tore the rifle from his shoulder, took aim, and fired twice in succession. Slobodan collapsed on top of the old man, and the two of them lay motionless. Mrs. Krkljuš tried to throw herself on her son, but at the sound of the shots a group of soldiers came running and formed a circle around the bodies, threatening to shoot anyone who came near, and Mr. Krkljuš and Aca caught her and held her back from certain death. The column moved forward, closing ranks around the corpses and rendering them invisible. Mr. Krkljuš and Aca propped up the sobbing, semiconscious woman and led her forward, step by step. They were numb now and cured of all illusion: they were being thrust into an abyss of pure horror; they no longer noticed what was going on around them.

The roar of a motor approached, and a car full of officers sped past the column, raising great clouds of snow. It pulled up in front of the changing sheds. A few people in the column stood on their toes to get a better view. Soon everyone, prompted by the excited whisperings of the few, followed suit and saw the officers jumping out of the car and going up to the patrol commander, who gave a stiff, nearly trembling salute. The officers exchanged some words with him, and he turned in the direction of the beach and disappeared in double time behind the white cabins. The people in the column failed to grasp or dared not hope what the commander's disappearance might mean until they heard "Left turn!" and the order to return to town.

They ran. They ran and pushed and shoved and sobbed—old men, old women, women with children in their arms. They ran, leaving the now silent beach behind, avoiding the corpses strewn along the roadside. Mrs. Krkljuš tore out of the crowd and flung herself on Slobodan, who was lying on his back at the edge of a ditch next to the old man, whose hat was now resting on his chest, courtesy of one of the soldiers, but the column forced them on, and the guards shouted threats, and Mr. Krkljuš and Aca again grabbed her and rejoined the running crowd.

They ran until they reached the Cultural Center building, where the soldiers tried to reassemble them. But the people bounded up the steps, stormed the door, and crowded in to where it was warm, human, familiar, dropping to the marble floor as if it were soft and comfortable. Soon loudspeakers above their heads began to buzz, and someone made a deliberate, formal statement to the effect that the raid was over, many dangerous elements had been uncovered and duly punished, and the citizens present there had been found innocent and would therefore continue to enjoy their constitutional rights and were free to go home.

A murmur of disbelief soon turned into cheers and applause. People hugged one another, kissed one another, wept, dispersing slowly at first, then with greater urgency. The Krkljuš family wanted to find an official with whom to lodge a complaint about their grievous loss, but, swept along by the crowd, they were unable to stop until the exit, where a soldier was trying to keep order. The soldier refused to listen to them and even threatened to shoot if they did not leave immediately. And in fact sporadic shots could still be heard. Mr. Krkljuš and Aca looked at each other, then took Mrs. Krkljuš under the arms again and led her down the stairs, promising that the moment the shooting stopped, they would go and find Slobodan's body. The promise could not be kept, however, because that very night the army collected all the corpses in the city, including those on the road to the beach, and either buried them or threw them into the Danube. All that remained were the bloodstains, and they only until the next snow.

The Mercury, like all buildings on the side of Old Boulevard with odd numbers, fell under jurisdiction of a search patrol led by Police Lieutenant Nándor Varga, the tall, young, blue-eyed scion of a landowning family. A gambler and drinker and man of limited intelligence but strong convictions, Varga scorned the plebeian awakening of his people under German patronage and resisted it with lordly arrogance. Throughout the raid he strictly followed the regulations he had sworn to uphold and therefore sent for further investigation only those civilians whose papers and oral statements failed to satisfy those regulations. The general's reproaches, which Varga's meager reports gave rise to every evening, he heard out at attention and in silence but drew no moral from them, convinced that they did nothing to preserve order. He had sent none of the hundred or so motley residents of the Mercury for further investigation, but that had been partly the doing of Predrag Popadić.

What happened was that on the morning of 21 January, when news of the curfew spread among the residents, two early risers, Doselić the pharmacist and Kreuzhaber the furrier, ran into each other in the corridor and, having exchanged a few words of alarm, decided to turn to Popadić on the third floor for an explanation and for protection: he was close to the regime yet a Serb and a gentleman. They had to ring his doorbell a long time: Popadić had been up until dawn at a patron saint's day celebration (Saint John). Nor was he alone but with the young grass widow of a restaurant owner, a Serb conscripted to a labor battalion. Popadić had been caught unawares by the news of the raid, but no sooner did he learn of it from Doselić and Kreuzhaber in his entrance hall than he grasped its scope and significance, remembering the talk of reprisals that had been bandied about in official circles during the previous few days. He also foresaw the unfortunate consequences that could result should the woman in his apartment be discovered and her presence there wrongly interpreted. He assured Doselić and Kreuzhaber that he would put in a good word for them, sent them on their way, woke the young woman and told her to get into her clothes, shaved and dressed in haste, and went downstairs to see the custodian, who along with his large family (a wife, two sons, a daughter-in-law, and a grandson) were also up and about. He drank the black coffee offered him (the custodians all loved him, big tipper that he was), smoked a cigarette, and shared a few comforting words with some tenants who had come to find out what was going on. The custodian's younger son, who had been sent to keep watch in the corridor, ran in to report that the police were at the door.

Popadić threw on his coat and hat and thus appeared in impeccable civilian attire before Nándor Varga as the custodian let the policeman in. He bowed, raised his hat, introduced himself in fluent if somewhat rough Hungarian—which Hungarians from the mother country, in Varga's case at least, smiled upon as the attempt by a savage to acquire the rudiments of civilization—and begged Varga's kind permission to present some documents of a rather confidential nature that might facilitate the delicate operation Varga and his men were about to perform. The lieutenant gave an impassive nod and agreed to leave his men in the corridor and enter the custodian's parlor. There Popadić took the following documents from his pocket and one by one handed them to the lieutenant: a letter from the commander of the gendarmerie authorizing the publication of *Naše novine* under his, Popadić's editorship; a pass granting Popadić free movement throughout the occupied southern territory; and finally—what really won Varga over—membership cards for two closed societies: the Catholic Circle and the Association of Christian Merchants. Taking advantage of the impression he saw he had made, Popadić requested permission to say a few words about the Mercury's residents. They were all, he was firmly convinced, the most loyal and devoted of citizens; he was willing to vouch for each of them personally. The lieutenant smiled, raised his fine eyebrows, handed him back the papers, and coolly invited him, if he so desired, to accompany the patrol and make certain it did its work correctly. Thus Popadić became a participant in the raid (which, as some wicked tongues later had it, made him a traitor), though in the unconventional role of protector.

Before each door, Popadić managed to find something positive to whisper to the lieutenant about the tenants, in the vein of the human-interest story, which he had long ceased to write but which his optimistic nature continued to inspire. Then he would retire to the far end of the corridor or terrace so as not to disturb the men in the performance of their duty or to overstep the bounds of decorum. He reentered the conversation only if a problem arose: a document wanting, an inappropriate answer because of inadequate linguistic knowledge. Blam—who answered the doorbell, deathly pale, together with a wide-eyed, incredulous Janja—Popadić described to the lieutenant as the offspring of an honest family he had known well before the war, "one of those young Jews able to adapt: witness his choice of a Christian spouse." When they came to the third floor, Popadić unlocked the door to his own apartment and urged the lieutenant—though by then they were not only colleagues but, he hoped, friends as well—to go ahead, to do his duty. The lieutenant thanked him, walked into the entrance hall, gave it a perfunctory glance, and came out with a smile, saying that unfortunately he hadn't time for a proper visit, but once his tiresome obligations were over, he would definitely give him a ring. (He was in fact true to his word.) Popadić bowed and moved on with him. After seeing the lieutenant and his men to the main door, which the custodian, crossing himself, locked after them, Popadić returned to his apartment, where he found his sweetheart perched on the edge of the bathtub in her coat and scarf, pressing her black patent-leather handbag to her breast.

# Chapter Twelve

Lili Ehrlich sent a number of letters to Blam after the war, but since she addressed them to Vojvoda Šupljikac Square, where other people were living by that time, and because she wrote the name of the addressee in its German form, Blahm (the letters were in German), none of them were delivered; they all went back to the sender marked Unknown/Inconnu.

The following are Lili's letters, in translation:

*Tivoli near Rome, 1 November 1944*
*I am writing this letter, darling, in the hope it will reach you, which will mean that you have come out of these awful years alive. How could it be otherwise? You'll let me know at once that my intuition hasn't deceived me. You will, won't you?*

*I can't believe that it's over, that I can move about, breathe freely, that I'm no longer threatened with death or persecution. We've had an exceptionally beautiful autumn here. It's not the slightest bit cold. The leaves in the many parks are just beginning to turn. Papa and I walk for hours through the hills surrounding the town. Yes, I need motion and freedom: we spent the last four months in a camp. We didn't have too bad a time of it, but barbed wire everywhere you looked—that I will never forget. Now we have private accommodations, but Papa still brings home food from the camp, where he gives English lessons. You know how capable he is. He gets so much food, we can give* some to our landlords, an elderly couple that might otherwise starve to death. Try to picture them: he a retired professor of literature who has been totally blind for eight years, she reading him his favorite authors, Dante and Tasso, every night by the oil lamp (we have no electricity). I often sit and listen, and though I don't understand a thing, I enjoy the melody of the marvelous language.

Write back the minute you receive this, darling, and pack your belongings. I don't know whether you were wrong not to come with us four years ago. Maybe you were spared many of the trials we've gone through, but don't think twice now. We're free here, and I await you with open arms. I long for you as I never have before, though I've done nothing else these four years. I will never, can never forget the days we spent together, and although we were on the run, Papa and I, and in danger, those were the most beautiful days of my life, and all thanks to you, darling, to your warm eyes, your quiet smile, your restless hands. I long to have you by my side, I long to touch you, hold you. Come!

I don't even ask if the others are alive and well. Uncle Vilim. Aunt Blanka. Estera (who is no longer a little girl, I'm sure). I'm selfish, I know. I think only of you. I love you so much.

Come, come at once! Or at least let me hear from you! Send a telegram if you can!

> Hugs and kisses from your impatient
> Lili

Tivoli near Rome, 26 December 1944

Dearest,

I can't tell you how crushed I am: the letter I sent you two months ago came back the day before yesterday. What can that mean? That you're out of town? That you've been deported and haven't returned? That you've moved? I don't dare think of all *the awful things likely to keep me from finding you. I will simply keep looking tirelessly, undaunted, until I succeed. I've been told I can send this letter via the Red Cross and that the American forces are helping people to locate lost relatives. You can be sure I will try everything. But if you receive my letter first (because things may have changed in the meantime), let me hear from you at once.*

*Yours,*
*Lili*

*Biel, 23 March 1946*

*Dear Mirko,*

*It's been raining for days, and I sit here in despair. Perhaps I have no right to despair, perhaps I'll suddenly find some trace of you, but when, I wonder, when? I keep thinking of the past, the irretrievable past. I think of my dear mother, who died so young and full of life. I think of you, who filled my life with love for one brief interval and whom I left behind. Why did I leave you? Why must I leave everyone I love? Why does my hunger for life, for survival, keep me from happiness, which, brief as it may be, is possibly worth more than the life now facing me?*

*I fear the life now facing me. It is a cold life and will grow colder. Perhaps the cold comes from Switzerland with its mountains covering the sky, its endless winter rains, its dull, sober people who know nothing of warmth, desire, and love. Every other week we are visited by an immigration office official who gives us forms to complete, the same forms each time. Where and when were you born? Why have you entered the country? How do you make your living? Do you plan to stay? If not, when do you plan to leave? Do I plan? What do I plan? The only thing they don't ask is whether I plan to kill myself and if so when and in what manner?*

*Forgive me for writing you my dark and jumbled thoughts, darling. It's not so bad. We're fine. Papa has a job in a local sewing machine factory. He is well paid and well respected, and we have everything we need. We've taken a beautiful apartment, and soon we're going to buy a car (a used car for now), which means we'll be able to wander to our hearts' content.*

*Spring is in the air, I can feel it in my bones, and maybe the reason I'm so out of sorts is that it refuses to come. I do so need sun and motion! And I need you, my darling! You have no idea how much I think of you, how often I dream of you, dream of you coming to me—sometimes with a slightly ironic smile because I'm so impatient—and embracing me as you once did. But then I wake up and I'm alone, you are not next to me, and I realize I don't even know where you are and am haunted by thoughts of the most terrifying possibilities. Forgive me, but what can I do? The letters I sent you from Italy (you still don't know where we were when the war ended) were returned to me, and all my inquiries through the Red Cross and the embassy have been in vain. Still, I will never, can never believe that the end has come. No, you are too much a part of me, we are two halves of a single body, and one part cannot be separated from the other without the other's knowing it, feeling it. You're alive, aren't you? You'll let me hear from you at once. You will, won't you?*

*I haven't the courage to finish and send off this letter. It's been sitting on my desk for three days now. Do you see what I'm afraid of?*

*The weather is nice. There is dew shining on the grass when I walk Papa to the factory in the morning. Each time I come home, I think I'm going to find you in my room, just sitting there and smiling. I'm writing these last lines in a café, and I'll rush home as soon as I send off the letter. But even if I don't find you there and even if this letter too comes back, I'll write you another and another and I won't stop until I've found you.*

*I want you to know that, if you receive these lines. Ever, any-
where. I shall always wait for you. Write me at once.*

*Yours,*
*Lili*

*Hamburg, 7 June 1949*

*Dearest Mirko,*

*I've decided to write to you immediately because I'm happy,
and superstitious enough to hope that one happy event will lead
to another. I arrived here yesterday from Biel, and right after
breakfast—because I had a nine-o'clock appointment—I went
off to the Grammophongesellschaft, where I had a personal in-
terview with the head of production. Papa has invented a kind
of filing cabinet for records. I don't know how it is in Yugoslavia, but here record collecting is all the rage and people are
making record libraries the way they used to make book libraries. Anyway, Papa has come up with a system of shelves that
allows you to choose the record you want to play by pushing a
button. It took a lot of work (and money) to perfect it and put
together a prototype in a factory in Bern. But now we're out of
the woods! The man I spoke to has expressed interest in manufacturing and marketing the "Ehrlich cabinet" and is drawing
up a contract that will give us 1.5% of the profits. (Papa isn't
feeling well, which is why I'm here on my own, but I'm sure
that as usual it comes from his working too hard and that the
good news will put him back on his feet.)*

*I was so excited and happy when I left the Grammophon-
gesellschaft office that I had the sudden feeling I was going to
find you, so I made for the nearest café to write to you again. I
simply can't imagine that this letter will fail to reach you now
that after all these years of deprivation we have finally latched
on to something solid. Actually we made a big mistake by not
coming straight to Germany after the war. We both knew it, we*

*even talked it over, but whenever it came time to take the final step, one of us would find some "but," which as you can guess always boiled down to the fact that we had suffered so from Germany and the Germans. Now that I'm here, though, I see it's the only place for us. There's nothing to remind us of the old hatreds. The people I meet on the train, in the street, the Grammophongesellschaft—they're all so open and optimistic and full of energy, and even though there's rubble everywhere, there's also building everywhere, the streets are full of life, the shopwindows full of goods, the service in taxis, on the phone, and in cafés is excellent. And the language! After all that murky Swiss dialect I am finally hearing the pure, flowing German my dear departed mother taught me. I feel revitalized, reborn.*

*You must be laughing at me, darling, because you know I'm over the hill, getting on to thirty like you. Our age is one of the many things we have in common. But the love that binds me to you is as strong as it ever was, perhaps because it has gone unused, unconsumed for so many years and therefore remains as tender and young as we were then. Now I'll be able to love you full strength, so to speak. Now that we're mature and have been through so much.*

*But here I am sad again, ready to burst into tears. I think of you as my child, to clutch to my breast, to warm and nourish, but I have no child, my child was lost to the world, torn out of me, torn out of me by these very people, maybe by the waiter over there with the scar on his forehead, the one watching me out of the corner of his eye. Where are you, darling? Am I ever going to find you? If Papa and I move here—and we've got to, it's the chance of a lifetime—years and years will go by before we get German citizenship and I have the right to travel freely and look for you. Or will God have mercy and will you answer this letter? My heart is pounding like a hammer at the thought. I can just picture you receiving it, coming home and picking it up, opening*

*it, smiling, nodding, and ten days later I have your answer.*
*Don't worry, even if we leave Biel for good, I'll leave a forward-*
*ing address with the landlord. He's very trustworthy. Your letter*
*will find me. I'll tell everybody and leave the address at the post*
*office too. All you have to do is write! Then we can talk it all*
*through. There must be a way to bring you here. Don't worry.*
*I'll see to everything myself, because my only desire is to have*
*you here by my side, for good, till the end, till death, my only*
*love, my husband, brother, and son. You are everything to your*
*loving*

*Lili*

*P.S. Write at once. Even if your life has changed and my out-*
*pourings sound odd to you. Just let me know you're alive. I*
*leave for Biel in an hour and a half to give Papa the good news*
*and wind things up there.*


*West Berlin, 25 June 1951*

*Dearest,*
*I met a Yugoslav here today, a nice person with a lot of go, a*
*businessman who has come to set up a diplomatic mission. Natu-*
*rally I was thrilled to learn where he came from, and I took the*
*first opportunity to tell him about you and about my unsuccess-*
*ful attempts to establish your whereabouts. He gave his word*
*first, to pressure your diplomatic representatives, with whom he*
*has close ties, into moving the search forward, and then, when*
*he gets home (in seven weeks), to mobilize his friends in Novi*
*Sad and let me know the moment he finds out anything about*
*you. You can imagine how excited I am. No matter what chan-*
*nels I try—diplomatic, commercial, military—all I get are*
*promises. Maybe personal contact will break through the wall of*
*indifference. The moment this ray of hope appeared, I just had*
*to sit down and write to you, as I have so often before and as I*
*would do much more often were it not for the fear of failure,*

*which unfortunately so far seems justified. In any case, here is my address, and the moment you receive this letter (if you receive it), let me know. And of course let me know if Herr Momir Stoikovitsch—that's the name of the nice businessman—finds you seven endless weeks from now. I've loved you and waited so long! I have no one but you. Papa died last year of a heart attack. I'm all alone in the world. I'm in Berlin now. I run a small jewelry shop. I don't own it, but I make enough to live on. Enough for us to live on, at least for a while. But what does that matter. Just let me know you're alive.*

*Love,*
*Lili*

# Chapter Thirteen

I wish I'd put my galoshes on," Blam thinks under his umbrella, watching the raindrops sparkle on the semicircular tops of his black shoes. He wriggles his toes and feels the moisture seeping through the shiny patent leather and into the loosely woven fabric of his socks. He meditates on the futility of the layers in which man chooses to wrap himself, on how poorly and provisorily they protect him from the wet, the cold or heat, and the wind: all they need is a slight detail of the unforeseen—like having to stand in the rain at a burial service—and they fall apart and leave him in the hands of the enemy. He twists his head and, peering under the rims of umbrellas crowded together like bats, finds the coffin, now nailed shut and covered by a black pall embroidered with a silver cross, on its bier in front of the chapel. The body of Aca Krkljuˇs, lying in it motionless, washed clean (Blam saw his face in the chapel; it was free of blemish), would soon, the moment it was deposited in the moist earth, begin to unite—through the invisible pores in the wood and the glue, through the holes made by the nails, through Krkljuˇs's clothes and the entire fabric of his body—with the cold, black, slimy juices of nature, eaten away by them and eating away at them.

Blam shudders, but at his own frailty, not his friend's. He cannot grasp Krkljuš's frailty, whose death he still perceives as an external matter: an unexpected turn of events, or the dive of an acrobat that is cause more for amazement or admiration than for horror. He feels the need to join the funeral procession, to tug at somebody's sleeve and mention a fact that may finally make sense of the acrobatic feat. "I saw him only a month ago. He was in perfect health, full of plans . . ." But he senses that it would sound like a cliché, and besides it is all wrong, because what was unusual about Krkljuš's fate was not so much the short transition between health and death as the transition itself, the complete surprise of it. When he hears the word "hospital" in the whispering of two former schoolmates (his and Aca's) in the row in front of him, he moves closer to their wet coats.

"It was his liver," the thin, stringy-necked Tima Spasojević says in his bass voice, leaning over the curve in his umbrella handle to Dragan Jović, who is shorter than he.

"No, jaundice," Dragan counters immediately. "I have it firsthand. My brother-in-law's a doctor. There's been a regular epidemic lately, he says. Krkljuš didn't have a chance. Two weeks, and he was done for."

A murmur runs through the front rows of the crowd, where people are most closely packed. Through the swaying umbrellas Blam can make out the pale, redheaded priest appearing on the threshold of the chapel, followed by the unshaven sacristan holding an umbrella over his head. The procession moves forward. The priest throws back his head until his sparse, reddish beard sticks out horizontally. He rounds his lips, puffs out his chest, and releases a solemn, stately chant that the gap-toothed sacristan joins and doubles in a bleating voice. The murmur dies down at once, and several thin, wailing women's voices come to the fore. From the archaic but clearly enunciated words of the chant, though even more from the sobs that it calls forth, Blam concludes that the priest is bidding farewell to the deceased in the name of the mourners. Although he too is deeply moved by the terrible finality of the farewell, he is overcome by embarrassment when he notices people all around him crossing themselves. Blam looks at them furtively and wonders what to do: if he joins them, they may think he is a hypocrite showing off his last-minute conversion; if he does nothing, he will seem to be demonstrating an obstinate fidelity to his former and very different faith. Yet there is nothing of either faith— former or new—in him: apart from a general superstitious fear of death he cannot recall a single detail of either of them, a single detail of the ritual. The last time he was at a funeral was when his grandmother died and he was only a child. All his other relatives disappeared at the same time and there were no funerals.

He suddenly wonders—he has never thought about it before—whether a funeral has any meaning, that is, whether there is any real difference between being buried or not being buried, between being tossed nameless and alone into the mute maw of nature and this group farewell with chanting and wailing, so solemn, so formal, a combination of invoking the deceased, taking leave of him, and perhaps even longing to join him. Of course, symbols have a calming effect on both the dying and those who mourn them, but Blam is not interested in psychology; he is interested in the existence or nonexistence of an essential difference. Would he feel different about his parents, about Estera, about other relatives, or friends, like Aca's brother, Slobodan, if they were buried here, in a cemetery, rather than having been tossed into a pit somewhere? Nor is he interested in the comfort that comes of a place you can go to once or twice a year or every month and mumble a few prayers—or not, if you are atheist, as he is. No, he is after something deeper. Would they seem more real to him if he knew where they lay? No, not seem, because that would mean going back to illusion and deceit. Would they *be* more real? Would he be able to derive strength from them, or would that strength be self-deception? Illusion, illusion everywhere, even in this painful question! He tries to picture their graves—stone after stone, all in a row and surrounded by grass—and himself standing and facing them, but it gives him no insight. They are silent now, like Aca Krkljuš, though it happened long ago and long before their natural time, though what is natural time, if Aca reached his because of a congenital disease or drinking too much? Death could easily have come to him earlier, if instead of his deaf brother he was the one to kneel by the old man who fainted, or if his section of the column had simply reached the Danube before the order to stop was given. He would have been just as dead as he is now, but an older corpse, eaten away by the water, the slime, the fish, while today he is being turned over to the descendants of those fish who were deprived of his body then. Or, rather, to those worms. Fish or worms—is that the only difference?

The umbrellas in front begin to sway again, breaking the raindrops' monotonous fall, scattering them this way and that; the coffin under the black cloth bobs a little in the hands and then on the shoulders of the four pallbearers, floating in the air under the crowns of trees whose green merges with the white, gray, and pink rocks of the woods ahead. The people are confused when the procession makes a turn, but the priest rallies them, showing them the way, and moves on with the sacristan in a slow, dignified pace behind the coffin. They are followed by two hunched women in black, Mrs. Krkljuš and a relative (or a neighbor, if she has no relatives), and two men in black coats supporting them under their elbows, then two more men and two women. Old Mr. Krkljuš is not among them; he is at home, Blam assumes, too weak to move. Blam pictures him slouching listless in his chair, his head sunken on his chest, his eyes fixed on the floor, eyes that think rather than see, think of what is happening to his son, though the old man may have made his peace by now with not seeing the reality of his son in the hospital bed, ill and dying. Aca was simply taken from him one day, and now Mr. Krkljuš no longer has him; Aca went almost as fast as Slobodan all those years ago. Mr. Krkljuš has never seen Slobodan's grave, and he will never see Aca's; he seems condemned to his chair forever. So the murdered and the dead by disease can end up very much alike.

Blam trudges after the procession, at its tail end, slowly, because the path between the graves is narrow and people keep joining it on all sides. He comes up to Spasojević, who has been separated from Jović by the crowd, and nearly bumps into him, and although he and Spasojević have recognized and greeted each other before, Spasojević holds out his hand and, raising his black, almost false-looking eyebrows, says with a sigh, "I bet you didn't expect it either. Our ranks are starting to thin now too, so it seems."

Blam nods, though his thoughts are still dwelling, almost longingly, on the comparison of different yet identical deaths. "It started a lot earlier," he wants to say, "with Slobodan and Čutura," but he is afraid it would sound like a boast or a hint at the sacrifices his own family has suffered—if Spasojević knew about them, that is—so instead he decides to say something that is in fact a boast and a hint at his own circumstances, though more in keeping with the occasion.

"I went to see him a month ago. He asked me to come."

Spasojević is taken aback: his eyebrows go all the way up to his hairline, and he stops in his tracks.

"Who? Aca?"

Blam nods.

"Yes. We sat next to each other in school, remember?"

"I remember, I remember," Spasojević says, passing over Blam's explanation lightly and moving on to what really concerns him. "But that means he was perfectly healthy!"

"Yes, perfectly healthy," Blam says, "and even full of plans for the future." But he suddenly feels terrible going on about things so obviously of concern only to them, the living.

"No one can tell what's happening inside," he hears Spasojević say just as he is separated from him, mercifully, by the procession, which has now paused and is spreading along the narrow pathways between the graves.

The coffin with Krkljuš's body first rises in the pallbearers' arms, then sinks to a pile of freshly shoveled earth. The coffin is yellow against the black walls of the pit around it. They swiftly and skillfully push it onto the two thick ropes that have been thrown across the pit and, releasing the pressure on them evenly, ease the coffin down into the earth. The priest and sacristan sing out in full voice; the two women wail. The shorter of the two bends over the grave, and for a second the veil reveals the delicate profile of Aca's mother. She makes as if to hurl herself onto the coffin, but the two men in black have anticipated her move and grab her arms. The priest raises his voice almost threateningly, and the sacristan not only follows suit but also points his umbrella with unexpected bravado at the sky and pushes his tinny voice a third octave above the priest's. The people around the grave bow and sprinkle the coffin with handfuls of earth, which hit the wood with thuds reminiscent of distant cannon fire. Now everyone seems in a hurry. The pallbearers, their hair dripping with rain, grab shovels that lay hidden behind a tombstone or tree and briskly, energetically fill in the grave.

This is the end. Aca Krkljuš is now exactly what he would have been had he not returned from the Danube, and what Blam would have been had he remained with his family in the house in Vojvoda Šupljikac Square, had he not been so taken with Janja or perhaps with the salvation he sensed in her. Was it worth it? Inhaling the moist air redolent with freshly dug earth, drawing it deeply into his lungs, he feels it was: life is wonderful, sweet, fragrant, palpable, engrossing. He feels a thrilling, irresistible impetus in the cold contact of the raindrops on his neck, feels it in the sticky soil that cools the soles of his feet through the stiff soles of his shoes, feels it in his frozen hands that seek warmth in the pockets of his coat. Death is terrifying no matter where and when it comes, and life, though it brings us closer to death with every instant, is wonderful.

ČUTURA DIED ON the day he left Blam's Dositej Street love nest, having locked the gate behind him as he was told and having left the gate key and door key in the place agreed upon. He set off early in the winter dawn and by half past six was on the road to Bačka Palanka, where he was to find refuge with a miller whom he did not know but whose name and address he had been given. He moved quickly along the firmly packed snow on the right-hand side of the street, but stopped whenever a horse and cart came up behind him, raising an arm to beg a ride. But, given the dangerous conditions of the area and the not particularly prepossessing picture he made in his floppy hat and threadbare city coat, the peasants would turn their heads the moment they saw him and even whip their horses to get past him as quickly as possible. He also attracted the attention of two gendarmes patrolling the area between the railway barrier and the hemp factory far out in the fields: the way he kept raising his arm and his brisk, determined gait made them suspicious. They waited behind an abandoned woodpile and then set out after him, shouting, "Halt! Halt!"

Čutura stopped, turned, and stood where he was until they reached him. They asked for his identity papers, and he showed them a work certificate that had been made out to a butcher's apprentice in Palanka. They asked him where he was going; he said he had spent some time in the city and was on his way home to work. They ordered him to raise his hands, unbuttoned his coat, and searched his pockets and trouser legs for weapons. As he had been required to hand over his pistol to the contact who gave him the false work certificate the day before, they found nothing. He could therefore assume that they would let him go.

But although their search had been unsuccessful, they remained suspicious, because two days earlier, in connection with preparations for the raid, they had received strict orders, which neither Čutura nor his contact could have known about. One of them blew a whistle, and the figure of a noncommissioned officer emerged from the hemp factory. The whistle was a signal that the two of them would be leaving their post. They then placed Čutura between them, slung their rifles over their shoulders, and set off for Bačka Palanka.

Čutura was well aware that in Palanka his work certificate would be proven false, that he would be taken into custody, and that because he was on the wanted list, he would soon be identified. He naturally regretted having given up his pistol and halted at the gendarmes' command, but it was too late to escape now: no matter how fast he ran, their bullets would catch him within fewer than twenty paces.

But after they had been walking for a quarter of an hour and came to two bare poplars at a bend in the road, where the first houses of Bačka Palanka showed through the snowy mist, the chance for escape did present itself. One of the gendarmes, short, squat, and somewhat asthmatic, asked the other, the one with the whistle, to stop long enough for him to light a cigarette. The three of them stopped, and the short gendarme let the rifle slip from his shoulder into the crook of his elbow to free up his hands. True, the other gendarme moved back a step and aimed his gun at Čutura, but the short gendarme had trouble getting to his cigarettes—he kept them in the jacket of his uniform, underneath the strap of his knapsack—and since his fingers were stiff from the cold and he had to twist and turn his body to reach them, his rifle started swinging back and forth. At one point the tip of the bayonet grazed the gendarme's fleshy, red double chin, and Čutura kicked the butt as if it were a football, sending the blade deep into the man's jaw. The man screamed, threw open his arms, and fell backward, but Čutura grabbed the rifle before he hit the ground, aimed it at the other gendarme, who was staring terrified at his mate, and put a bullet through his chest. The second gendarme fell flailing, and Čutura leaped over both bleeding bodies without a moment's hesitation, the smoking rifle still in his hands, and fled in the direction of Novi Sad.

But the small, round gendarme had only been lightly wounded; he was more concerned with having nearly been killed by his own bayonet. Seconds after his head hit the snow, his mind cleared and he felt around for his gun. When he failed to find it and caught sight of Čutura running off, he realized the man was escaping with it. He turned to the other gendarme, whose death had taken place in the short interval the small gendarme was unconscious, and saw him stretched out in the snow, his gun at his side. He struggled to his elbows and, paying no attention to the blood streaming down his neck and dotting the snow, crawled over to it. Knowing it was loaded, he scrambled into shooting position—legs spread wide, elbows firm on the ground, right shoulder steadying the butt. He was a good shot, and only because he was in too much of a rush did the first bullet miss its target. The second time he aimed slowly and calmly and hit Čutura just below the right shoulder blade. Čutura twitched, shook his head, losing his black hat, and slipped. He seemed certain to fall, but managed to keep on his feet and even made a half turn, as if to return the gendarme's fire. Then, clearly lacking the strength to do so, he hunched forward and continued in his original direction, not running now but lurching from one foot to the other, his knees buckling with each step. The gendarme cocked the gun and aimed carefully again, this time hitting Čutura in the small of the back, in the spinal column. Čutura twitched once more, less violently, and after two short scraping steps toppled headfirst into the snow.

Shortly thereafter two gendarmes from the hemp factory, alarmed by the shots, appeared on their bicycles, pedaling strenuously through the loose snow. They stopped just short of Čutura, jumped down, and approached him, guns raised. Čutura was lying on his side with one cheek resting on the snow and his eyes closed; he might well have been sleeping. They turned him on his back. Tiny opaque bubbles of blood were trickling from his mouth. One gendarme stood watch over him while the other ran over to their injured comrade, who had managed to get up on his knees and was pressing a handkerchief to his wound. He helped him to his feet, and together they went over to the man Čutura had shot. He lay there dead, white, his palms upward, seeming to beg, his eyes open, glassy. The gendarme who had helped the wounded man up asked him if he could hold out until first aid came, and when the latter nodded, the gendarme went back to Čutura, jumped on his bicycle, and rode off to Palanka for a car. By the time it arrived, Čutura had died without regaining consciousness. They loaded the two bodies into the car, and the wounded gendarme squeezed in at their feet, still pressing the blood-soaked handkerchief to his ample double chin.

"Are you Leon Funkenstein?"

"I am. What can I do for you?"

"I need to talk to you. But not here in the hallway."

"Come in, then. Here, have a seat. What can I offer you?"

"Is this your apartment? You live alone?"

"Yes, I do."

"Sorry to be so forward, but it's not an idle question. Have you always lived alone, or did you by any chance lose your family?"

"I have nothing to hide, even though I never saw you before in my life. Yes, I did lose my family. And given my name, you can pretty much guess why and how."

"Did they die in a camp?"

"Some did. Of my immediate family of four, three died in a camp: my mother, my wife, and my daughter. My son froze to death doing forced labor in the Ukraine. Of my extended family of nineteen, thirteen died in camps, two were killed during the raid, one was hanged at the very beginning of the Occupation for supposedly having opened fire on Hungarian soldiers, one aunt died here at home after being tortured, and one nephew poisoned himself just before he was to be sent to a camp."

"You keep a careful record, I see."

"You know how it is. You have them on your mind, and you go over and over them through the years. At some point you decide to sort them out."

"Sort them out? Why? For revenge?"

"Revenge? Revenge is for the authorities."

"And if the authorities fail?"

"If the authorities fail, we as individuals are all the more powerless."

"That's not completely true. Surely you've heard of the agency in Vienna that tracks down war criminals. It's run by a Jew. The one who brought Eichmann to trial."

"You mean Wiesenthal? Wiesenthal is an important man, an expert with a worldwide network and lots of money. We little people can't do anything."

"You can't do what he's doing, but on a limited, personal scale . . ."

"I don't see how. Do you expect me to find the gendarme who packed me off to the camp? The officer who put my son on the forced labor list or chased him into the freezing cold? They escaped, they're in hiding. Or they've been punished by now."

"But you're looking at an isolated case, your family's. What if I pointed out men guilty of making Jews suffer? Would you help to see them punished?"

"I . . . I don't think so."

"Why not?"

"Because it's none of my business. I'm in real estate. It's not my job to catch and punish criminals. Let the people who are paid for it do it."

"And if they don't? If, say, they can't take up a certain case?"

"What kind of case?"

"This one, for instance. A highly respectable Jewish family has a tenant, a widow, whose lover, a scoundrel and Arrow Cross member, has moved in with her. Comes the raid. The Jews have already lost their Communist daughter in a skirmish with the gendarmes. The patrol naturally quizzes the man about the Jews, and on the basis of his information the family is sent to its death. There are no witnesses of what he told the authorities, of course, and no way of protesting: he would simply deny everything. But his physical presence in the house on the day of the Jewish family's death is proof that he denounced them. All that needs to be done is confront the man with his crime, and he'll confess. Would you help in a case like that?"

"I might, but what could I do? I'm just a little man, an ordinary man. Weak, and old now too. I can't cross-examine anybody, much less force a confession."

"You wouldn't have to. I'd take care of that. All you'd have to do is get him to go with you to an inconspicuous place outside town, where the cross-examination and punishment could take place."

"But why me? Why would he come with me and not with you?"

"Because you're in real estate, because you were the agent for the sale of Vilim Blam's house, the house this man was living in when he committed his crime. You can introduce yourself as the only living witness of the transaction and promise him a reward if he goes to a nearby village with you and makes a statement. He'll agree to it because he needs the money: he drinks. He won't tell his wife about it so she doesn't find out about the money."

"You're asking too much of me. What makes you think he'll trust me enough to go with me? And how can I get him to a nearby village without being noticed?"

"I'll show you a tavern to go to, a place where no one will notice you. You have a way with people. He won't think twice about going with you. He'll be attracted by the reward, and his guilt feelings will do the rest. You'll invite him for a little spin—to Kać, say—and provide the car and driver. I'll be the driver. That's all you need do. I'll make sure that the man who has a score to settle with him—Vilim Blam's son, that is—is on hand when we drop him off. If nothing else, you'll see justice done. After so much injustice. It's time, don't you think?"

# Chapter Fourteen

It rains all day. The raindrops fall from the clouds, now tepid, now cold, now straight, now at an angle, in thick jets or one by one and big as bullets. They fall, splattering on roofs, walls, gates, and windowpanes, singing in tin gutters, drumming on roads and pavements, watering the earth, filling its invisible crevices, finding faulty joints between tiles and bricks, seeping into walls and leaking into cellars and basement flats, whipping faces and necks under umbrellas, soaking, drenching, dissolving form and meaning, people and things.

Or the wind blows, biting and dry, mean as a lynx, sweeping dead debris—dust, trampled refuse—from cracked earth and faded asphalt into windows, under doormats and doors, down noses and throats, making people cough and choke, tearing posters from poles, bending trees in parks, and rattling the craftsmen's tin signs till they squawk like frightened poultry.

Or it is a magnificent summer when nothing moves, neither air nor earth nor azure sky, neither the burning sun nor the shadows it casts on the streets, and the people walking, the cats stalking the pavement, the ants crawling through grass seem unreal and unnecessary in the general torpor of heat and fecundity.

Or it snows, a blinding blizzard, rooms heated desperately hot, people rushing down streets, shoulders hunched and teeth chattering, slipping, falling, breaking bones, but then the clouds disperse, leaving a sugar-white cover, smooth as silk, pure as milk, soft as wool, until frost grabs and chains it, turns it into a wrinkled gray skin that stops outstretched fingers from piercing warm earth, tree roots, flowing waters, until the south wind and the thaw take pity and steam rises like a heathen prayer from the earth, dissolving the cold weight that rests on the streets, squares, houses, and people and planting on them and in them new strength and new colors.

And because rain, wind, sun, and snow all take place in the city, the city seems created to accommodate the seasons, to serve as a retort for testing the fiber of man and material under varying conditions of pressure and temperature. The city is not an element in the broad scheme of change, no, it is a discrete granule, a richly variegated granule, and while the same might be said of the sea, the woods, or the mountains, the city is unaware of belonging to a whole, even the whole that is existence, so when city people say to one another, "It's hot" or, "The wind is blowing," what they mean is that it is hot or the wind is blowing here in the city and that they have revised their image of the city—the streets on which they live and the people with whom they live—accordingly.

WHEN THE DEFEATED conquerors left Novi Sad in October 1944, they left not only with the jewels, furs, and rugs they had plundered but also with hundreds of accomplices who, suitcases in hand, stole out of the back doors of the apartments and houses they had confiscated. Predrag Popadić was not among them. Had he forgotten to reserve a place for himself in one of the military vehicles, as people later speculated, or did he simply go on believing in his luck and perhaps in favors for services rendered to the underdog? Or was it that he could not bear to part from the city that had afforded him so comfortable a routine, so beautiful an apartment, a standing window-table reservation at the finest coffee house, a multitude of women he had bedded and intended to bed, and so many suits of expensive material and silk ties and soft terrycloth robes that not a tenth of them would have fit in a refugee's suitcase? The fact remains that he had published *Naše novine* as long as the paper supply lasted, and that the days immediately before the Soviet and Partisan troops entered the city he had spent indulging in the other side of his life—paying visits, giving and taking advice, making new acquaintances and deepening old ones, holding dinner parties and keeping amorous assignations—the side of his life he had always considered the more important.

On liberation day—liberation from his superiors and therefore from himself—he had sense enough to remain alone at home, sending the custodian's younger son out twice for provisions and looking out his large windows at Main Square, which was now packed with crowds of people hugging and kissing, waving flags, tossing flowers to soldiers, singing, firing cannon salutes, dancing the *kolo*, and cheering. Cheering in Popadić's native tongue, which for three and a half years had been condemned to whispers, lamentation, or lying. Perhaps it was the cheers—so innocent in their exuberance, so of a piece with his pleasure-loving nature—that overcame the voice of fear the very next day and led him among the people. Or perhaps he was made bold by the lonely night after that lonely day, a night of bitterness and temptation, a night without human contact, without warmth, without conversation, without news, yet within arm's reach of all these ingredients of life so essential to him.

In any case, the next morning he bathed, shaved, put on his Sunday best and a light gray overcoat and hat, and stepped out into the street. He made his way to the curb, mingled with the crowd, felt on his face the breath of the cheering men and women, watched the People's Army parade past, the jubilant young peasants in carts drawn by spindle-shanked horses decorated with banners and foliage. Soon acquaintances started turning up in the faceless throng. When Topalović, a wine and cheese merchant with a goatee and suspicious little eyes, to whom Popadić had given his business, sidled up next to him, all moroseness and concern for his shop, Popadić tried rousing him with a smile and some words of praise for the hale and hearty youth all around them. Topalović rewarded him by bleating the latest gossip into his ear, namely, who would be heading the municipal council, whose wives had agreed to take in which officers, and, incidentally, the fact that Popadić's former underling, Većkalov, had been seen at city headquarters hobnobbing with the high command. This piece of information led Popadić to make a fatal move: even though Većkalov had worked at the paper as a proofreader for only a month and a half, having lost his job as a teacher with the coming of the Occupation, Popadić assumed he would be grateful to the man who hired him in his hour of need, so he took his leave of Topalović and headed straight for Town Hall.

There, amid the whirl of men and women sporting uniforms, cartridge belts, and five-pointed stars, doors opened surprisingly fast before Popadić's anomalous appearance, the military authorities responding to his queries politely though not quite knowing what to make of him and therefore sending him from room to room. Popadić came upon Većkalov in a small office on the third floor. Wearing a uniform, a partisan cap, and a new, dark handlebar mustache,

Većkalov was attended by three men in mufti scraping and bowing before him. Većkalov gave a start at the sight of Popadić and immediately cut short his conversation with the civilians, who eyed the newcomer inquisitively as they filed out.

"What in the world made you come here?" Većkalov shouted the moment they were alone, shooing Popadić to the door with both hands the way one chases away chickens or ghosts.

But Popadić stood his ground and smiled. "I just wondered whether I could be of any use to you."

"You must be out of your mind!" Većkalov bellowed, horrified, and rushed to the door. "Leave this instant!"

Popadić wavered, the smile frozen on his lips, but Većkalov flung open the door and cried out in a voice meant to be heard up and down the corridor, "Leave, I tell you, or I'll call the guards!"

Popadić turned white, put on his hat, and left.

Back in the square, he stood lost in thought for a while, jolted now and then by the crowd; then he turned and headed slowly home. Just as he reached the Mercury, a young soldier with an automatic rifle over his shoulder approached and asked, "Are you Predrag Popadić?"

"I am."

"Then come with me."

They walked along Old Boulevard—Popadić smoking a cigarette he had just lit, the soldier pointing his automatic at Popadić's left side—accompanied by stares from passersby. Suddenly Miroslav Blam appeared.

"Wait a second!" Popadić called out to the soldier and took a step in Blam's direction, as though he wanted to explain what had happened, but the soldier immediately grabbed his arm and yanked him back to the curb.

"You go off again like that and I'll shoot," he said, looking Popadić in the eye and giving him a poke in the ribs with the rifle.

Once he had regained his equilibrium, Popadić took a careful look at the soldier. Then he shrugged, bowed his head, and set off, leaving Blam looking amazed, compassionate, and relieved all at once.

Just beyond the Mercury they turned down Okrugić Street, which was deserted, passed a number of houses, and came out on Old Boulevard again. They crossed it and took Toplica Street to the former Jewish Hospital, which the Hungarian army, upon occupying the city, had emptied of patients and made into a barracks. Now it was swarming with partisans, and a partisan with a rifle standing guard in front of the wire fence nodded to Popadić's escort and let them in without a word.

They went into the courtyard, passing two tarpaulin-covered trucks, and entered the building through a kind of vestibule, the waiting room of the former hospital. The walls were still lined with white benches, though they were now occupied by young partisans cleaning their weapons and chatting quietly. At the far end of the vestibule a capless, middle-aged partisan sat at a small table that clearly did not belong there. Clouds of cigarette smoke, mixed with loud voices that seemed to be quarreling, wafted through the half-open door behind him. Popadić's escort led Popadić to the table, where the stern, ill-tempered partisan took his identity papers and entered the necessary data into an exercise book that lay open in front of him. Then he ordered him to empty his pockets and went through the contents for a long time, returning everything but the wallet and the pocketknife.

A phone rang behind the half-open door, and someone

picked up the receiver and spoke. Suddenly the voices in the room fell silent, and a thin young curly-haired partisan wearing an officer's uniform with no insignia appeared in the doorway. He looked around the vestibule and went straight up to Popadić.

"Are you Predrag Popadić?"

"I am."

The officer gave him a surprised, then a bemused look.

"The editor of *Naše novine*?"

"Yes."

The officer nodded and with a finger summoned a soldier on the nearest bench. The soldier jumped up, quickly reassembled the automatic that had been in his lap, and ran over to the officer.

"Room 6," the officer said, giving Popadić another curious look. Then he turned and went back into the room, shutting the door behind him.

The soldier with the automatic took Popadić by the arm. "This way," he said and led him down a long, well-lit corridor where several other soldiers were walking up and down with guns over their shoulders or at their chests.

"Room 6!" he called out with the same bemusement as the officer, and one of the soldiers turned and unlocked a door. Popadić's new escort took him to the door, poked him in the side with his rifle, saying, "In you go," and Popadić crossed the threshold.

He found himself in a large bright room full of people sitting on the floor. There was no furniture. He stood for a moment, stunned by the sight, but when the key turned in the lock behind him, he moved forward, careful not to step on anyone and searching for familiar faces. It was easy, because everyone was looking up at him. He immediately found several acquaintances and waved to them, but the figure that attracted his attention most was one huddling next to a closed window covered with curved wrought-iron bars. It was his political editor, Uzunović. He made his way to him, barely maintaining his balance, and held out his hand.

"What's going on here?"

Uzunović shook his long, mournful head.

"They're shooting us."

"Impossible!"

Looking around in disbelief, Popadić saw someone beckoning to him. At first he thought of going over to the man, but when he saw it was Sommer, the German lawyer who had served on the Raid Commission Board in 1942, he simply waved back and sat down next to Uzunović.

"Maybe you've got it wrong," he said in a pleading voice. "They'll have hearings first, investigations."

Uzunović shook his head again.

"No hearings. Just firing squads. You'll see."

He closed his eyes and dropped his head between his knees. Popadić lit a cigarette and stopped asking questions.

From time to time the door opened, and a new person was pushed in by an unseen hand or entered reluctantly on his own. He would look around and either find someone he knew or remain standing by himself, but after switching from foot to foot for a while, he would eventually be humbled enough to find a place on the floor. The short autumn day soon came to an end, and since there were no lights and space was so tight, people started bumping into one another and quarrels broke out. The air grew heavy, and an irritated voice asked for a window to be opened, but when people sitting near the window tried to open it, it turned out to be nailed shut. Others went to the door to ask permission to go to the toilet. No one seemed to pay attention to them, but after a long while a guard opened the door and shoved in an old bucket. The pilgrimage that ensued cost many their places on the floor, but indignation was to no avail. No food or drink came, and no one thought of asking for any. Popadić held off going to the bucket until evening, when the stench reached even his spot near the window. By then people were stretched out—some drowsing, others merely exhausted from the ordeal—and he had a hard time making his way there and back. He returned to find Uzunović in a heap, his mouth wide open, sound asleep. Popadić crawled over to the wall next to him, thrust his hat under his neck for a pillow, leaned back, and soon dozed off himself.

He was awakened by a commotion at the door. It was open, and a ray of light from a giant battery-powered light cut through the darkness. Behind it he could make out a tall, broad-shouldered partisan in a well-preserved German uniform shouting, "Silence!" though there was nothing but a low, sleepy buzz of voices in the room.

"If I call your name, go out into the corridor," the partisan said in his resonant voice, enunciating each syllable. "Do you understand? Only if I call your name. Nobody else."

He lifted a piece of paper to the light and started reading names. He called out each name loudly and clearly, then repeated it softly, as if to himself, until someone pulled himself up from the crowd and pushed his way over to him, past his massive body, which all but blocked the doorway, and out into the corridor. After the partisan had read about fifteen names, he lowered the paper and the light and left with no explanation. The door closed behind him; the key turned in the lock.

Questions like Who? Why? How? surged from the lips

of those left behind, because they all tried to guess from the names on the list what was in store for them. Their speculations were cut short, however, by a voice in the dark warning them to hold their tongues, and as they slowly, begrudgingly complied, they heard a motor revving up outside. "They're taking them away," someone muttered, expressing aloud what they were all thinking. It was the last comment of the night. The noise of the motor had made it clear that their fates were being decided not here but in a place they could not see, could not know, could not even fathom. All they could do was whisper their lamentations and final messages to one another. Some who had been particularly uncomfortable tried to find better spots for themselves; others stretched out again. Popadić remained against the wall, smoking.

That night, three lists were read. Uzunović and Popadić were in the third. After squeezing past the partisan in the German uniform, they were immediately seized and shoved roughly against the wall by young, sweaty soldiers. When the partisan had finished reading the names, he counted the men and shouted, "Right face!" The soldiers hurried them out one by one into the courtyard, which was pitch black except for an occasional flash from the partisan's light, and over to a truck whose back gate was down. Two soldiers hoisted them up and jumped in themselves, and someone on the ground pushed the gate back in place and fastened it with chains. Then the truck gave a rumble and jerked into motion, making a broad circle.

Popadić wound up in the middle of the truck, and all he could see over the heads of his companions and from under the tarpaulin was a cloudy night sky without a single star. He had no idea where the truck was going, particularly as its headlights were off and it kept changing direction.

Finally it slowed down and began to bounce through a series of potholes that sent its human load rolling across the wooden floor. The soldiers rattled their guns and ordered their charges back to their seats. Then it stopped, and the motor fell silent. There were voices outside, people calling to one another. The chains were undone, and the gate fell with a bang. The soldiers jumped out and ordered everyone to follow. The prisoners were surrounded by another group of soldiers—six, all with guns over their shoulders—then forced into a column, two by two, and pushed past the truck through a thicket.

It was perfectly still except for the swish of their footsteps in the wet grass and the rasp of their breath, heavy from running. The air around them was motionless, and the trees stood out clearly against the dark gray of the sky. Then there were fewer trees and the column came out on a small clearing just as the horizon turned white and the first rays of the morning sun pierced the woods beyond and fell on the finely rippled surface of a broad body of water. They realized they were on a bank of the Danube. The soldiers called them to a halt. All around, the prisoners heard branches cracking, saw shadows flitting and human figures stirring among the trees. The soldiers in the escort left them in the middle of the clearing, moved back to the trees, and unslung their rifles. A man emerged from the shadows behind them, a short, thin man dragging his right foot and holding a double-barreled gun like a hunter. He went up to the column and waved the first two men forward a step, and when they complied he raised his gun and fired twice in a row. The men fell to the ground, moaning. Then he pulled the bolt back, and the cartridge cases fell out.

"Who wants to be next?" he asked in a high voice.

The light was growing stronger, coloring faces and clothing, and it was obvious by now that the man with the double-barreled rifle was very young, his chin smooth, his round, pug-nosed face the face of a child, though disfigured by a bright red scar that stretched from the left ear to the middle of the chin and had not quite healed. Limping along the column, he stopped at Popadić and cried out in his singsong voice, "Well, well! What have we here? A real gentleman! Who might you be?"

Popadić gave his name.

"And how many Communists did you shoot?" asked the young man in a low voice, as if confidentially.

"None," Popadić answered.

"None, you say. But you lived it up while we died, you dog!"

His voice cracked, and he raised his arm and knocked the hat off Popadić's head.

"Step forward!"

Popadić stepped out of the column.

"I have a special bullet for pretty boys like you," he said, and stuck his hand into the pocket of the jacket hanging loose on his sunken boyish chest. After fumbling a little with the pocket, he came out with a long, pointed metal object and thrust it into Popadić's face.

"Know what this is?"

Popadić shook his head.

"Well, it's a dumdum bullet, and when I plant it in your wavy locks your own mother won't recognize you. You understand?"

He hobbled a few steps back, inserted the bullet carefully into his gun, and took aim.

"Mouth open!"

Popadić looked confused.

"Open your mouth, damn you! I'm going to shoot you in the mouth!"

Popadić opened his mouth.

"Wider!"

Popadić opened his mouth as wide as it would go. The young man pulled the trigger. A shot rang out, and Popadić's head burst apart. Thus pruned, his body stood straight on its legs like a tailor's dummy for an instant. Then it slumped to the ground.

"Here we are, gentlemen, you can both get out."

"Here?"

"Yes, here. But mind your feet. The ground is uneven."

"I'm sorry, Mr. . . . What did you say your name was? I thought we were going to Kać for me to give testimony. This is a swamp."

"The name of the man you are addressing is Leon Funkenstein, but do not blame him for ending up here instead of at Kać. It was my idea to bring you here. I am responsible for everything. I, Ljubomir Krstić. Also known as Čutura."

"But why?"

"You will know soon enough. We need one more person before we begin. Let me see if it is time. Half past six on the dot. I am now going to whistle. Don't be alarmed. It is a signal we once used in school. There. I hope that Blam is where I arranged for him to be and will soon appear."

"Who?"

"You heard me. Blam. Oh, don't start shaking. You are not going to see a ghost. I do not mean the late Vilim Blam, whose house you inhabited illegally. No, it is his son I have in mind. Miroslav Blam, alive and well, husband and father, gainfully employed."

"What are you driving at, Mr. . . . ? I have no . . ."

"I told you Funkenstein has nothing to do with it. And don't try to run. I've got you where I want you. And you're not so strong as you used to be, Kocsis. That is your name, is it not? Lajos Kocsis? . . ."

"It is, but I refuse to . . ."

"You cannot refuse anything once you are in the power of another. You've known that truth for a long time now. Since the day you joined the Arrow Cross. No, quiet! I think I hear something."

"Help!"

"Shut up, you fool! One more sound out of you and I'll twist your neck, not your arm! Can't you see you're trapped?"

"No violence, please, Comrade Krstić!"

"You keep quiet too, Funkenstein. Now would you look behind those bushes and see if Blam is coming? And hurry him along if he is."

"He's coming."

"Good. This way, Blam, this way. I want you next to me, both of you. You will now join me in judging this bastard, who, as you can see, would do anything to get away from us."

"Mr. Blam!"

"Mr. Kocsis. I'm sure I don't know . . ."

"Well, I'm sure you will as soon as the trial begins. Lajos Kocsis, you stand here. In the name of this citizen's court I hereby accuse you of having denounced and defamed Blanka Blam and Vilim Blam, the parents of Miroslav Blam, here present, on 22 January 1942, as a result of which they were shot to death. You are therefore an accessory to their murder. I recommend that you be shot to death. Are there any questions?"

"But that's . . ."

"Just a minute, Blam! I think we should give the floor to the accused first. Have you anything to say for yourself, Mr. Kocsis?"

"This whole thing is a farce! I don't know what you're talking about! I never denounced anybody!"

"Is that so? Then I'll have to refresh your memory for you. Fact by fact. Tell me, do you deny that on 22 January 1942, the second day of the Novi Sad raid, you were in the residence of your mistress, Erzsébet Csokonay, number 7 Vojvoda Šupljikac Square?"

"I do not."

"And do you deny that on the aforementioned day a patrol of gendarmes and soldiers entered the aforementioned house and carried out several searches?"

"No."

"Do you deny that the patrol entered the Blam residence first?"

"No."

"Do you deny that after searching the Blam residence, they entered the residence of Erzsébet Csokonay?"

"No."

"Do you deny that the patrol leader asked your opinion of the Blam family."

"Yes! Yes, I do!"

"Nonsense! You're lying! Which is the clearest proof of your guilt! All the patrols questioned their countrymen about people of other nationalities. Now you tell us what you said about the Blams to the patrol leader, Kocsis, or else!"

"I didn't say a thing, not a thing! I swear! I said they were fine, upstanding citizens."

"You're lying again, Kocsis! Which confirms our worst

suspicions. Because if that was what you said, the Blams would be alive today. Alive, understand? Their death is proof of your crime."

"I didn't do anything."

"You caused the death of two innocent people! You fanned national hatred, intolerance, blood lust, racial insanity; you sought revenge and booty; you aided fascism to cut down two of its opponents. In their name and the name of thousands of other raid victims I pronounce you guilty and sentence you to be shot to death. Here is a pistol, Blam. You will carry out the sentence."

"You must be crazy!"

"Take the pistol, I tell you. Take it and shoot him. Don't be afraid. Nobody will ever know."

"Have pity on me!"

"Yes, Čutura! Let him go. Please let him go."

"It's too late. We'll end up in prison if we let him go now. Shoot him, I tell you!"

"I can't."

"You're the only one who can. And you must. You're the only one free of guilt: Funkenstein and I lured him here under false pretenses. We could be arrested. So you've got to shoot. If only for our sake."

"I can't."

"Look, Blam, I'm warning you. This is your last chance to be a man. Either you kill him, or I hand the pistol over to him and have him kill you."

"I can't."

"Is that your final word?"

"It is."

"All right, then. Let's see what he wants to do. Here's the pistol, Kocsis. It's loaded. Shoot Blam."

"What for?"

"It's the only way you can stay alive. Shoot Blam. Good. Shoot him again. I can't believe it. You killed him, and it only took you two bullets . . . You know, Kocsis, I'm beginning to respect you. I even think you've earned the right to live."

# Chapter Fifteen

Blam is listening to music. He is leaning back in his seat in one of the middle rows of the Novi Sad synagogue, completely at ease, surrendering to the tones that enter and pervade his being like a second bloodstream. The melody caresses, quivers, thunders, evoking images that to Blam's captivated mind appear random, even chaotic, but are in fact causally connected. He sees himself running bare-armed and bare-legged through a gently undulating meadow into an evening still sunny yet cool; he feels the tall, firm grasses lashing against his calves, while from a distance comes the ringing of bells, spurring him to run faster. It is the memory of a late summer spent in the mountains, when school had begun but he was convalescing after a bout with pneumonia. He encounters a hazy warm female whose face he cannot see but whose breath, sweet as anise, he can smell. He sinks into a raging torrent, leaps into towering, chalk-white waves, struggles, rises and falls, but never tires, merely fades into the roar tearing him apart. He is perfectly aware that these images are no more than the play of his senses, because his music-glutted senses continue to deliver—with less force, perhaps, though with equal clarity—information about his surroundings: the domed space high above, the rows of benches filled with hushed people, and on the altar, now a stage, the musicians with their instruments, the Novi Sad Chamber

Orchestra, producing the notes and through them the images, emotions, and thoughts. He can even, should he so desire and without abandoning the play of notes he has succumbed to, follow the course of their making: the conductor waving his arms, the string players hunching over their violins and cellos, the wind players puffing their cheeks out and running their fingers over keys. He can pinpoint odd, amusing details: the trombonist assiduously licking the mouthpiece before putting his pursed lips to it in a kiss, or the long-armed, bald cellist carried away by the rhythm and swaying to and fro like a pendulum, or the conductor going up on his toes, spreading his arms wide and, when his tails fly open, revealing a tightly trousered backside. Ever the observer, Blam takes it all in, but, as always, from a distance, coldly, avoiding the standard reactions of laughter, anger, or malice— as he avoids them in everyday life, because he senses, knows, that this too is a game. Everything here is a game: the powerful tones, the musicians who create them, the audience, the space provided for the music, even the inner experiences triggered in him by the cumulative effect of the notes. None of it is, as in life, irrevocable, fated. For such is the collective covenant, the ancient, mythic, everlasting covenant: that the magic of a harmonious progression of notes should transport us into the world of our impulses and injuries, and that we are unafraid of being led astray by the former or trapped by the latter, like a dream made to order, a dream whose course we ourselves direct.

THE STRING OF notes comes to an end with the end of the piece, and the magic is rent by silence. But then applause breaks out like a death rattle or like the wail of a newborn wrenched into the world and knowing instinctively that by gaining a full, independent life it is losing the warmth of its mother's womb. The warmth fades: up on his podium the conductor turns to the rows of benches, bows, wipes the sweat from his low forehead and fleshy cheeks with a handkerchief, then gives the orchestra the signal to rise and share in the honors. Here below, the people clap, leaning over to one another and exchanging impressions, or stand, impatient to leave the place of harmony destroyed. For they sense that what they are leaving behind is not the musicians but the music, their common cause, without which both performers and audience are superfluous.

Blam applauds as well, then rises to go out for the intermission. His seat, only a few moments before a haven of secret meditation, is now just a space on a dark-brown wooden bench, angular, hard, coarse to the touch. Moving away from it, he inadvertently bumps into the people inching along ahead of him, and he finds that human contact as distasteful as the contact with the bench. Both are prisons. The people moving along the rows are no longer a faceless crowd drawn here by the rules of music; under the harsh light of the chandelier, their bodies take shape, their features become recognizable: they are now Dr. Such-and-Such and his wife, and that young man with the long hair, he is Professor Futoški's son, and over there is a man whose shop Blam sometimes patronizes, and if Blam greets him, he will activate the workaday shopkeeper-customer relationship, and the man may well ask whether Blam was satisfied with his latest purchase of lemons or soap.

To escape that danger, Blam bends his head and gazes down at the feet of his fellow citizens, which he is less likely to recognize than their faces, and hopes that he is less likely to be recognized. But just as he is about to leave the row, what should appear before his lowered eyes like a fish from turbid waters but a beaming, round, shiny face, its eyes wide in joyful recognition. Funkenstein! Is it possible?

Yes, it is none other than Leon Funkenstein dressed in black from head to foot, standing there waiting for him, hands in pockets, stocky short legs spread wide, firmly planted in the aisle that most of the people are taking to get to the vestibule. There is no trace of the amnesia Blam met with in the Main Square that summer. Funkenstein is festive in his stiff black suit with its somewhat overbold white stripes and white, bannerlike, breast-pocket handkerchief.

"I kept wondering if it was you," he says, holding out a warm, fleshy hand. "I don't believe I've ever seen you at a concert before. Are you a music lover? Are you by yourself?"

Blam answers in the affirmative, though vaguely, because he is not certain exactly what he is agreeing to in Funkenstein's outpouring, and Funkenstein takes a ceremonious step back and bows ever so slightly but purposefully, to make room for Blam rather than to let him pass.

"I adore music!" he announces too loudly, lifting his face to the glittering chandelier, the gilt drapes gracing the walls, the colorful windows reflecting the artificial light against the dark of the night. "I've loved it since I was a child. We were poor, you know. My father was a feather merchant, and there were six of us. But we each had a hobby. Mine was music. Our religion teacher—Jolander was his name, you wouldn't remember him—played the violin, and I decided I would too." He clicks his tongue in fond remembrance.

They have passed into the vestibule with its four white marble pillars supporting the choir loft. Funkenstein looks around cheerfully and says, "I think we can smoke here."

He takes a flat silver cigarette case out of his breast pocket, obviously placed there for this occasion. When he opens it, Blam sees that the inside is tarnished and the rubber bands holding together several spindly cigarettes amid much loose tobacco have lost their elasticity.

"Cigarette?" he asks, and when Blam declines and takes out a pack of his own, he lights Blam's cigarette and one for himself with a lighter that has suddenly materialized in his hand. "We have time for a stroll," he says, setting off at a brisk clip through the clusters of people, as if Blam's acquiescence were a foregone conclusion.

Blam can do nothing but follow. Funkenstein stands out among the quiet people around them. Blam is put off by the man's raucous voice and finds his offhanded, pushy manner vulgar and unsuited to the ambience of a place of worship, which, though converted into a concert hall, has retained something of the sanctuary. Can he have adopted such a manner to show that he alone here is not an interloper? Blam senses that that is the case, and it only makes him more uncomfortable. It is as if the two of them have come to the synagogue with the express intention of demonstrating that it belongs to them, the survivors, as a disinherited landowner might visit a castle as part of a tourist group and at a certain point beam confidently and say, "Right! You've guessed it. This castle was once mine." It is as if they have come as a warning or even rebuke: "We aren't dead. Not all of us. Don't believe everything you hear. This is our temple. We feel at home here." Blam does not see how their presence as "former owners" can possibly go unnoticed. He has the impression that when the people around him lean over to one another, they are pointing out the two Jews huddled together, birds of a feather, a living reproach, a memento. He feels he has accidentally joined a crowd chanting a slogan he has no desire to chant and waving a banner—that defiant white banner of a handkerchief fluttering above Funkenstein's breast pocket with his every step—he has no desire to wave.

Funkenstein seems to be doing everything to confirm Blam's impression.

"That house of yours," he says for all to hear. "Where did you say it was? Masaryk Square?"

"No, no," Blam answers reproachfully. "Vojvoda Šupljikac Square. But that's over and done with."

"Why?" Funkenstein asks, stopping in his tracks and thereby making Blam stop with him. "Tell me. Why?" He starts walking again, mindlessly flicking the ashes of his cigarette on the mosaic floor. "Didn't you say last time that you had been forced to sell it during the war? Because of the Jewish laws or some such thing."

Blam blushes. He knows where the misunderstanding lies, but hasn't got it in him to straighten the man out. All he says is "No, we weren't forced into it at all. I only wondered whether my father was paid the money for the house."

"Money, money," says Funkenstein dismissively, completely abandoning the brash attitude he struck in the earlier part of the conversation. "How often we let it buy our silence," he laments, stressing the "we" to show he takes their common fate for granted. "But there are things money can't buy. We accept money as reparation for our suffering in the camps; we accept money for our families killed, for the experiments performed on us like guinea pigs. We're willing to turn anything into money. Even this temple." He turns on his heels, blowing a thick cloud of smoke up toward the vault, where colorful rosettes in round windows, blinded by the electric light, stare down on them. "We agreed to sell it. And who did we sell it to?

An abstract municipal entity that put the money into re-modeling and didn't pay us a blessed thing!"

"But there are so few of us left we couldn't possibly have kept it up on our own," says Blam, using the argument he heard while negotiations were still in progress. "Besides, it has wonderful acoustics, and now at least there's a place for us to hear music."

"Acoustics, acoustics!" Funkenstein waves what is left of his cigarette in the air. "What about the Youth Hall of the Board of Commerce where we had concerts before the war? It had acoustics, didn't it? And if the town fathers think a magnificent hall is so important, why don't they build one themselves? Because they haven't got the money, that's why. And you know why they haven't got the money? Because they haven't got the Jews to earn it for them!"

"Really, Mr. Funkenstein!" Blam admonishes. "You're going too far!"

Funkenstein frowns, then bursts out laughing like a child who has been found out. "You mean you don't agree?" And grinding his cigarette butt into the floor with his heavy shoe, he changes the subject. "So we're in business? We're going to do something about your house?"

"I really think it's too late. How can I prove my father didn't get the entire sum when I'm not even sure myself? And even if I could, what good would it do? The money is worth twenty times less today than it was then."

"You could have the house reevaluated," the ever practical Funkenstein points out. "You could claim the contract was broken and demand the property be returned to you. If you pay back the amount he received, you can resell it. Why not give it a try?" He pauses, then adds a provocative "You don't need capital, do you?"

"No, I don't really," says Blam with a smile, glad they have come the heart of the matter. "Here? Now?"

"The here and now means nothing to us," says Funkenstein, suddenly serious again. "We are here today and gone tomorrow." Again he puts a conspiratorial stress on the "we," lowering his voice and almost winking. "Who knows? Maybe you could get foreign currency for it. Maybe you could sell it abroad, in Israel, say. Do you ever think of emigrating?"

"Me? No."

"Well, I do. I'm seventy-three and have nobody left. I think about it all the time. But I'm accumulating my capital in goods, in books. That's right. Surprised? Well, I buy books, books people want to read—novels, stories, history, memoirs, mostly memoirs, the things our people abroad want to know about. Because if anyone starts coming after us again, I'm getting out, I'm going to Israel. If I can't die here, where I was born, I want to die in Israel— and books are something you can always take with you. They're not gold, they're not jewels, you don't need to declare them, and the moment I get there, I'll open a lending library for Yugoslav Jews. It's a going concern in Israel, did you know?"

In the heat of the conversation they have reached the entrance, its huge, dark doors open wide to the invisible night. They are the only ones there. Funkenstein takes out his cigarette case and lights up again. He tries the lighter three times before he can get a flame to last long enough— a brisk wind is blowing in from outside—but he scarcely notices.

"We're all so naive," he says with a sigh of resignation and expels another cloud of smoke. He has suddenly shrunk into a little old man, or that is how Blam sees him now that they are alone. Blam feels sorry for him, repentant now instead of shocked and resistant. Something in Funkenstein's words has touched him, something warm, intimate, a tone he has not heard in years, a long-forgotten spirit, a long-absent excitement, and suddenly a multitude of faces from the past floods his mind: his father sporting a mustache twisted upward, the calm and collected Ephraim Ehrlich, Lili. Lili is especially clear with her importunate "Come with us!" No one has invited him anywhere for a long time, and although he has no particular desire to go anywhere, his world is the poorer for want of invitation.

"How did you get through the war, Mr. Funkenstein?" he asks on impulse, sympathetically.

"How?" Funkenstein shrugs, not surprised by the question. "It was owing to what we've just been hearing, actually: music. My whole family, all seventeen of us, were sent to Bergen-Belsen in 1944. The head of the camp was known for his love of music. At roll call he asked who played a musical instrument, and I stepped forward. I was the only one who survived."

He gives Blam a penetrating glance, as if Blam, not he, made the statement.

"You know what my job was? I played for prisoners on their way to the firing squad. They would be loaded into a cart, always the same one, a children's wagon, a few boards on four small iron wheels pulled by prisoners. The condemned man would stand in the cart, bound hand and foot, and we'd walk behind him and play, me on the violin, Kohan on the trumpet, Eisler on the drum, though Eisler died early on and a youngster by the name of Gogo took his place. We kept it up for nearly a year, got better rations for it, and survived."

He pauses. But just then something squeaks. At first Blam thinks it is an instrument at the top of its register, then realizes it is a bell in the ceiling announcing the end of intermission. They turn back. Funkenstein flicks his half-smoked cigarette to the ground and steps on it with the nonchalance of a street-corner loafer. What opens before them, obstructed by the backs of the men and women returning to their seats, is the temple's elongated hemisphere, magnificently lit and dazzling in its gilt ornamentation, symbolic of the infinite vault of heaven or perhaps merely of the wealth of its former congregation or the desire for wealth on the part of those who conceived or commissioned it. Funkenstein looks puny and old under the vault. Blam pities him. The way he stamped out the unfinished, unnecessary cigarette makes Blam aware of how weak, half-formed, and unfulfilled Funkenstein is, the product of a small mind with large dreams.

"I'll let you know about the house as soon as I make up my mind," he says apologetically as they go off in different directions to their places.

BACK IN HIS seat, Blam tries to forget the whole incident. He settles in, crossing his legs and positioning his elbows on the armrests. The curtain parts, revealing the gold door behind the altar, and the first musician, a violinist, emerges, followed by the rest of the strings in single file. They are greeted by a muted, diffuse applause that increases when the energetic conductor, all smiles, makes his appearance. He mounts the podium, bows, and raises his baton for silence. Then with a subtle wave of the hand he calls forth, out of nothing, out of the void above the heads of the audience, a slow melody. Like many around him, Blam lowers his eyes to the program in his lap, recalling what he knew, namely, that he is listening to Dvořák's *Serenade for Strings*.

It begins dreamily, cajoling the emotions, pulling them into its wake. Blam follows its course, trying to submit to the flow like a swimmer leaving the shallows for the main current. But the melodic current eludes him: he is too aware, breaking it down into its components, its themes, and listening for individual instruments. He shuts his eyes, hoping to enjoy the music more, but even in the darkness under his eyelids he can see the musicians contributing their particular strands to the melody, the conductor signaling how and when to come in, the audience attentively following the torrent of their combined efforts, and himself among the audience, tense and overly sober, though seemingly in rapture. Yes, he sees himself clearly. It is as if another eye, a third eye, has opened within him or off to the side and is observing everything, independent of his will and the will of those around him. For a moment he thinks he has located the point from which the eye is observing, and since that point is more or less an extension of the bench he is sitting on, the bench he left at the intermission in the vain hope of remaining unnoticed, he has the feeling it is Funkenstein watching him. He opens his eyes and turns his head to the end of the row, expecting to find the pudgy old man in the black pin-striped suit and white breast-pocket handkerchief observing him. He sees no one. The bench is nothing but a row of heads facing forward, and beyond it there is nothing but the empty aisle and the wall rising rigid and solitary despite its golden scrolls and swirls. Then who is doing the observing?

The perplexity is unnerving. Blam feels certain he is being watched. He casts furtive glances to the right and to the left, but meets no eyes: all faces are looking forward, trained on the source of the music. Their concentration strikes him as curious, the concentration both of those sitting in the audience listening and of those sitting on the stage and pushing and pulling at their instruments to produce the desired sounds. And for what? For a bit of harmony, for the pleasure of it, for mutually agreed-upon oblivion, for the resurrection of images from the past or the unconscious. He cannot help thinking of the music Funkenstein has just told him about, the music that accompanied prisoners on their way to be hanged or shot. Was it to be hanged or to be shot? He did not ask Funkenstein, and that bothers him. The picture he has is incomplete; it breaks off at the most important point. Though he can follow it to that point. Funkenstein's story enables him to form a picture of the cart "like a children's wagon, a few boards on four small iron wheels" creaking sadly through a huge, barren courtyard ringed by barbed wire; of the men harnessed to it, practically skeletons, pale and emaciated, heads shaven, necks straining to move that vehicle of death, the guarantee of their survival to the next moment or next hour or next day; and of the bound man being sent to death for reasons unknown to him, swaying, staring at the ground or at the sky, the wire, at the feelings and memories evoked by the music. But what were they playing? Why didn't he ask? Maybe it was the slow movement of the Dvořák he is hearing now. Or Chopin's *Funeral March*. Or the funeral march from the *Eroica*. Though it could have been a cheerful, dancelike tune, because they were playing for the head of the camp after all, and he took pleasure in the executions.

Blam knows none of this; he had failed to ask. He had failed to ask not only Funkenstein this evening but also other survivors, eyewitnesses, books, just as he had failed to experience it himself! He had failed to face the rifle barrels like his father and mother, the search patrols like his sister, Estera; he has failed to go down to the Danube like Slobodan Krkljuš and bend over an old man on the ground, deaf to all warnings and moved only by the thought of the moment, the thought of assistance. He had seen nothing, learned nothing. And now he is turning to see whether an impetuous old real-estate agent is watching him. Because Funkenstein had experienced it. For an entire year he had played for bound prisoners going to their death, his violin under his chin, bowing carefully, making no mistakes, for his life depended on it. True, he survived, returned, he alone of a family of seventeen, but only after taking the risk, facing the truth, seeing, suffering.

Blam feels the invisible eye on him again. A reproachful eye. Can little Funkenstein, perched on a seat somewhere behind him, be concentrating on Blam telepathically? Funkenstein, who played for prisoners bound and condemned to death in a far-off camp, following their cart to the scaffold, and who now sits small and unnoticed in one of the last rows of his former temple, listening to the Novi Sad Chamber Orchestra because he "adores music"? Where does he find the strength? How can he sit calmly amid a rapt audience that, spurred by the music, spin the insignificant, selfish feelings they bring with them from safe homes and the bosom of secure families? How is it he does not cry out his truth? Blam pricks up his ears, but all he hears is the beautiful music. He lifts his head and scans the mighty walls, marveling at how high they rise over the benches, and at how small, how tiny the cluster of benches and the people on them are in comparison with the dimensions of the building. He wonders if the benches were made smaller during the remodeling to adapt them to the more intimate requirements of the concerts that would be replacing the more motley, less culturally diverse religious congregation. He cannot remember, he can only speculate. But the walls have remained as they were, that he can see— they account for the excellent acoustics—and they have retained their oriental swirls, tokens of a past with no continuity. The elongated Moorish cupola reaching to the heavens has remained as it was, the mark of a history of banishment and wandering; and yes, above the altar the two white marble tablets remain, the tablets on which in bulbous Hebrew script Moses received the Ten Commandments. How is it they were left there? For decorative purposes, most likely.

Now the remodeling, the compromise, looks inane to him or, rather, unreal, ghostlike. It makes him want to protest publicly, to shout out loud, perhaps, the way he expected to hear Funkenstein shouting from the last rows. He knows perfectly well that his religious feelings have not been offended: he has none. On the contrary, he senses from the nature of his anxiety that what bothers him are in fact the remainders of the religion. He is wounded by the past because he long ago rejected it, or wanted to. Childhood scenes, images he wishes to forget: his hand in the cold, firm hand of his grandmother taking him to this very temple for a holiday service; the wail of Levantine song coming from the cantor with the black beard and inflamed eyelids and wrapped in a thin linen prayer shawl; the buzz of prayer coming from benches crowded with the stiff black coats and hats of merchants, artisans, and middlemen; and upstairs in the balcony, where his grandmother disappeared after letting go of his hand, the busts of the long row of women hovering as if in a cloud, eyes troubled and shining, cheeks powdered white. Even then he felt a stranger to these displays of devotion and passion, because he sensed (prophetically) that on foreign soil, in a foreign world, this attachment to an ancient tradition with its Levantine songs and speech, feverish rituals, and a scintillating life of the mind made possible by distance and otherness could not survive, that it was doomed, condemned to hatred and destruction. Even then the dark, stifling atmosphere of bobbing bodies sheathed in stiff black cloth made him feel the need to break loose, to rend limb from limb, to spill blood, to flee. And flee he did, grateful for the enlightened atheism of his father, Vilim Blam, who himself gave the temple a wide berth, preferring the cosmopolitan smoke of the coffeehouse. But that too was self-deception, because for all his cosmopolitanism Vilim Blam ended up like the believers, his cosmopolitanism being in fact an integral part of their passion, their eccentricity, the eccentricity Blam so perceptively discerned in Lili, who was likewise forced to vanish from the stage.

They all vanished, thereby proving his prophecy, his premonition, his will. Yes, his will, because he had wished them to disappear, knowing it was inevitable and finding the wait for the inevitable to be excruciating. And so he had sought oblivion, an opiate to cut the wait short, as when he wandered the streets—visiting his parents and taking leave of his love for Janja—in the weeks before the raid, eager for death. Death was his goal as he roamed in search of something impersonal to mask his shame; death was what he sought here in the "acoustics," in merging with the crowd, losing his individuality and what was left of tradition and memory in the intoxication of the music.

But the music stops. There is a lull. The first movement is over. The conductor lowers his baton, takes the handkerchief out of his pocket, and wipes his neck and face. The musicians fidget. Then the conductor puts the handkerchief back in his pocket, raps the baton against the stand, and lifts it to begin a new melody in three-four time, polkalike or at least dancelike. Music for the head of the camp? Blam turns his head, almost expecting the new, livelier rhythm to move the people around him to something unusual, untoward, to release a drive that makes them leap from their seats and join hands in a ring or slit one another's throats. But nothing happens; they all remain seated, eyes riveted on the musicians. Their heads and nerves may be suffused with a desire for action and conquest and violence, but this is the wrong setting. A former place of worship lacking a congregation and possible victims is the wrong setting. All it is right for is rapture, hidden desire, and lies, a life of lies and half lies, the kind he himself leads. The pretense of life he has assumed after dodging death and saving himself, after pushing away all those hands stretched out to pull him with them—after pushing them into death. But the premonition, dodging, and flight have consumed him and robbed his life of meaning, leaving only stagnation and lies, a daze this side of death, but that side of life.

HE IS DEPRESSED. He has lost the need to rebel, shout, and show that there is no connection whatever. He has lost the third eye. The scene has returned to normal: an impressive hall with Levantine religious motifs, a stage where an orchestra plays, benches where an audience listens and enjoys inner experiences. Nothing more. A beautiful hollow space, an empty palace with a new purpose. The blood of the massacred has been wiped clean. Everything is clean, everything beautifully lit. There is nothing for him here.

Trained not to interrupt, he waits until the end of the second movement to take advantage of the short pause, rise—the noise he makes blends into the general murmur—and move toward the aisle. The people in his row make room for him, surprised; several stand, looking after him and whispering, but he is unperturbed, certain he will never again appear like this among them. From the aisle he heads for the exit, alone but accompanied by the music, whose lilting harmonies once more fill the void. The farther he goes, the softer it becomes; it is like an escort, like a pair of eyes resting on his back. Funkenstein's? He did not notice Funkenstein on his way out, but Funkenstein may well have noticed him, and he would have been as puzzled as the others. Though maybe not, if he had the same thoughts as Blam, if he knew what was going through Blam's head.

Out in the vestibule, at the makeshift cloakroom, Blam puts on his coat, half expecting Funkenstein to follow, to leave the hall and join him, though Blam does not want him to. He turns. No one in sight. Nothing but the glorious gilt-trimmed walls tapering into vaults around the cupola, and the music softly playing. Well then, he thinks with a mixture of relief and understanding, Funkenstein has stayed behind, the victim of his "adoration."

He passes through the wide-open door of the synagogue into the dark. It is cold, the wind is blowing, the streets are virtually empty. He heads for home, crossing New Boulevard at the blinking light and turning into what is left of Jew Street. Here there are a few strollers, couples, looking at shopwindows and clutching their coats and hats against the wind.

Main Square lies before him like a dark stage, the Mercury and the cathedral rising opposite each other in the background like a set. Lit only by the street lamps, they blend into the night sky, except for an occasional bright dot of a window. It is as though their tops had been destroyed, as though the terrible heat of a weapon had melted them and, upon cooling, they had taken on a new asymmetrical, ungainly shape, the shape of ruins. It is a scene from the coming war, the site of his future summons. "Miroslav Blam," they will say up in the mansard or down in front of the building or out in the square. Or they will call out a number they have given him. He will step forward and put his neck in the noose or take his place before the firing squad. He will not dodge death this time; he will close the circle he left open; he will enable a death to happen that must happen; he will reveal another murder, another murderer, another victim—in a man in whom they would not have been revealed, a man who might not even have seen them in himself—as all his people had done before him, thus committing, as he now realizes, an act of the most profound truth.